THE RAPE OF THE
VIRGIN BUTTERFLY

THE RAPE OF THE VIRGIN BUTTERFLY

a novel by

Valerie Kohler Smith

· THE DIAL PRESS · NEW YORK · 1973 ·

Library of Congress Cataloging in Publication Data
Smith, Valerie Kohler, 1934–
  The rape of the virgin butterfly.
  I. Title.
PZ4.S6589Rap [PS3569.M539]   813'.5'4   73–7767

For DG, the Bird, Butch,
Twank, and Morris

THE RAPE OF THE VIRGIN BUTTERFLY

· 1 ·

Ashley Dralon got back to the States they bought a six-year-old 1947 wood-paneled Pontiac station wagon and headed west to start in on yet another clean slate. Mort smiled a hairy, off-kilter smile, showing all his badly frightened teeth, and Ashley looked silently out the window. In the back seat a little boy, already too big, already too hairy, sat on *American Freedom and Catholic Power* and worshiped the back of his father's neck.

In the middle of New Jersey Mort drove right down the center of a block of freshly laid tar. The men who were having their lunches next to their still steaming handiwork jumped up and waved their Swiss cheese sandwiches at him while they cursed. Mort waved back.

"Golly Moses," he said to his wife. "It's good to be home. Look at all the friendly people." Then he sang, "I'll sing you one ho. What is your one ho?" and the oppressive weight of his tone-deaf voice lodged in Ashley's stomach like a strangled belch. By that time they were in Pennsylvania.

"Holy cow," Mort said, nudging his wife with his petrified elbow. "Look at all the foliating deciduous!" Then he turned to the open-mouthed boy to tell him about the turpentine, paper, rayon, maple sugar, quinine, and other useful products found in such leaf-bearing plants. His wife sighed, and Mort, with his mile-high, Trim-A-Comb crew cut, in his yellow crepe-soled Buster Brown stickball shoes (with the double bows through the brass eyeholes), who couldn't remember how old he was (thirty-three or six, in September 1953, when he was just thirty), drove on.

Mort and Ashley Dralon, on their way from Israel via Pier 57 to Frijolito, New Mexico, which means "Little Bean" and promised little else. Mort swore his teaching job promised a new life, but Ashley knew better. Ashley, with a red barrette in her fine, sandy hair, was from the Back Bay world of fine bone structure and had shown them all by marrying the son of a Jewish grocery store. Her fancy but Bohemian mother had advised her to screw her bloody head off if she must. "But for godsakes," she had said, "must you actually marry the yid?"

They passed Harrisburg.

Ashley patted her second pregnancy and sighed. Life

had so quickly gotten out of hand. Even her first-born, Rhile, had let her down, already waking up in the mornings with the scent of sour breath on his teeth. Getting away from her. Drawing her further into Mort Dralon's foreign net.

They lumbered on and on farther and farther west, and the station wagon smelled like an extra from *The Bicycle Thief,* just like her mother warned her it would. And not just the car. It seemed as if her whole life was littered with the contents of her husband's old knickers' pockets. Under her feet were three years' back issues of the Sunday *Times. The American Boy's Handy Book, Opera Librettos Every Child Should Know, With Malice Towards Women, How to Develop a Super Memory* by the renowned Harry Lorraine, and three jars of half-sour kosher pickles were stacked up behind her seat, so it was hard for her to get any clear view of what was either coming or going as they passed the Corinthian-columned post offices of Ohio, the pro-phylactic hillsides in Old Dutch Cleansered Indiana.

The father and son got out to make, and Mort's huge knapsack wallet hung down by the side of his leg like a swollen varicocele. He zipped his pants, cut slices of salami for lunch and wiped the soft globules of garlic fat on his bus driver's pants. Ashley watched him, wondering how she came to be with a tall, muscled stranger who seemed, way up there, to create his own weather. As they drove, Mort talked. The information he had all his life sucked up like a Hoover he now puked back verbatim, interrupting his monologue only to wave his arms around in ecstasy at the passing scenery, to explode with an occasional, "Criminetly, will you look at all that purple mountain majesty." Sometimes he'd wrench Ashley into his concrete ribs or tenderly rub her cheek raw with his barbed wire cheek. Ashley would murmur her "Uh huh," and suffer. The boy watched from the back seat in a state between shock and awe. And they drove on.

Often, Ashley pulled back and shook her head. She felt her eyes water and her vagina clench. She sat that way a long time, waiting and staring out the window. Mostly when Mort talked, Ashley waited. For foreign scenery to change, for boats to either pull in or out . . . for maybe only a state line marker. She waited for the baby inside her body to move, for her son's body to shift. For Mort to keep talking. Sometimes she waited as much as twelve hours for him to come back when he went to the store for a quart of milk. He'd get to talking. Or pass a book store, or maybe the guts of a lime green Studebaker to poke around in. It was good that she had come to him with a solid background in waiting. It had come in handy.

Indiana. Quiet. Yards, pitched roofs, parlor lights, and long, elm-dappled porches.

Mort felt the melting warmth of the Baby Ruths he had hidden in his inside pocket. Later, when Ashley wasn't looking, he would suck the sticky chocolate in through the cracks of his teeth. He knew sugar destroyed the calcium in the body, but what she didn't know wouldn't hurt her.

It was late when they crossed into Kansas, and Ashley drove. There was a silo on the left and a white farmhouse. A grain elevator and twenty miles of flat Kansas wheat land exactly. And then another and another and another silo, another house, and another grain elevator. Finally a sleeping white frame town and an International Harvester storehouse and then more houses, more silos, endlessly, forever. . . . Sometimes there would be a faint seventy-five-watt bulb in the distance and sometimes she could feel the bump of a railroad track pass underneath. Mort's sleeping mouth pressed open against the handle of the door.

He said that this time it was going to be different. Teaching the young of Frijolito. But one thing Ashley knew for sure was that nothing was ever the way you read about it in the travel folders.

· 2 ·

WHEN THE DRALONS HIT
Albuquerque they stopped to adjust their carburetor.
The mechanic stretched a greasy arm into the guts of
the Pontiac and screwed his neck around so he could
talk at the same time. "Gun it," he said to Ashley at the
wheel, and to Mort, staring out over the crest of the
valley with the sun in his eyes he said, "You folks stayin'
a spell?"

A spell? Were they stayin' a spell? Mort had never
heard such authentic western talk in his whole life. Of
course they were staying a spell.

The mechanic waved his screwdriver through the air
and told Mort that the old place wasn't nothin' much
in them days. . . . When he and his missus first come

along, he said. None of your fairgrounds, your drive-in movie theaters. And none of your secrets either, he said and Rhile looked up. He looked out where the man looked but all he saw was mountains.

"Yessir," the man said, and he rubbed the little boy's head. Then he winked at the father and went back towards the station saying, "Don't know but this whole damn town'd fall on its ass without them secrets, though." Rhile transferred his anxious eyes from the mountains to his father's face, but "By golly—" all Mort saw was the setting sun, and "Isn't it something?"

The mechanic came back to give Mort his change as a sandstorm suddenly began to blow across the mesa. Ashley had gone to pee and the little boy was still pulling on his father's pants. "What secrets?"

"Here it comes," the mechanic said, pulling up his collar. "Come back and see us, heah?" Then he went back inside the station and Mort, watching the sand move, thought that nothing in the world ever looked so much like Galilee. He was sure this time they had picked themselves a winner. The sand had already blocked out the volcanoes. Ashley had her hands up to her eyes as she hurried back to the protection of the car, but Mort pulled her to him.

"You are the rose of Sharon, my lily of the valley," he told her, but she pulled away, shrugging.

"Let's go," she said, "it's still sixty miles to Frijolito."

The sand had started as a whistling under the cuffs on Mort's pants, then increased in fury. Ashley struggled with the door on the station wagon but the wind was too strong for her. It stung her eyes. It spit down

· 9 ·

her throat. "Please, Mort," she said, "open the door," but Mort wanted to express in some small way the intense desire he had to pour out the innermost longings that welled inside him instead.

"I can't see where I'm going—Mort—" and the sand was hitting them like hypodermic needles.

"I want to go home," the little boy cried, and it was suddenly dark. No stars. No secrets. Not even his father's Gethsemane. Home? Mort couldn't even find the Pontiac.

"Stay still," he said. "Don't anybody move. I'll walk in a circle till I find either you or it, don't anybody move."

Don't worry, the boy was afraid he would fall off the end of the world and where could Ashley go? All around her was blinding nettles and lost way. . . . Airless, bleating heat stopped her breath. I want, Ashley moaned. Everything that's already gone and not in my cards, while Mort's voice, from the other side of a movie-set Sahara said something about north by northeast.

The sand beat against their eyelids with tumble-weeds and the feel of hot swirling grit got way inside the thick stitches of Ashley's 34A cotton and pigiron brassiere. "Here. Here it is," Mort called. He wrestled with the door with Goliath strength, got it open, turned on the brights so his flock could find their way in the dark and soon Rhile had forgotten about the secrets. They sat and waited for the sand to go as quickly as it had come. Rhile fell asleep. Ashley held her tongue and Mort must have shaken his head in awe seven different times. And then it was all over. They looked out the windshield and saw everything. The sand again as innocent as a beach. The quiet hung heavy and only bits of jetsam gave evidence to anything having ever been different. Mort started the motor and Ashley was all hunched up on the death seat like a baby sparrow too soon fallen from the nest.

They coasted down the long hill into Albuquerque past packing-crate housing developments, Eats stands and Conoco stations that darted in and out of the fading sand like strippers' G-strings. Mort reached for his helpmeet's hand but couldn't find it. He shifted instead into high and said, "Holy Cow, wasn't *that* ever something." Then all the way down into town he sang "Sweet Betsy from Pike," flat.

"No," Ashley said to herself when Mort first noticed the signs pointing to the university. "No," she said, "let's go on, it's still sixty miles." Her mouth was very narrow, and her voice was very narrow but it wasn't any use. He turned off Central at University Avenue and headed up towards the Administration Building. It was also Ashley who first saw the headlights bearing down too fast in the rear-view mirror, but it was Mort who first saw the kid in the orange ski sweater. The first things he saw was the argyle reindeer and second that the kid was tugging on a rope tied from one side of the street to the other (from the fireplug across the street, to the streetlight on this side).

"Now why do you suppose he's doing that?" he said, as he started to brake and brake fast. That was when Ashley tried to kick his brake foot out of the way.

"No," she screamed, "he'll hit us, the car behind. No," she screamed again, "and besides, there is no rope. The kid in the ski sweater doesn't have any rope———" She had seen that right away, but by that time it was too late. The Buick was in the trunk.

"Fucker," Ashley heard through the night. She watched the kid in the sweater pull back into the shadows and then gather up his imaginary rope. She recognized the whole pattern from the start—the old Halloween rope and the old Halloween trick. She wondered why Mort didn't.

The crash was loud and the Buick crumpled like an aluminum foil Easter hat. All of Mort's loose newspaper clippings and his shiny, striped suit pants were all over the street like a picnic after a cloudburst.

The initial thud sent Ashley onto the dash, Mort against her like a pile of dirty linen. Then she looked out the window and saw a very handsome, very blond, very burly college kid shaking his fist and cursing at them.

"Hey, four eyes," he was saying. She rolled down her window. "Nobody fucks with Billy Dawson! What the fuck do you think you're . . ."

She rolled it up again.

Mort didn't hear him; he was busy shaking his head back and forth from side to side, then in alternating arcs to make sure nothing was out of place. Then he went through the same routine with Ashley and the boy, who was still asleep on the floor of the back seat.

"Get outa that shit-turd you got there," this Billy Dawson was screaming at them. "Get outa there and look what that Okie wagon of yours has done to my Buick."

Mort rolled down his window and smiled at him. He said, "Hey there, son, now every driver knows the response . . ."

"Don't son me, you bastard," Billy screamed, and he waved his big blond fist in his face, so Mort turned aside to pick up *The Statistical Survey of the Serbian Economy from 1905–1927*, which had come apart on his son's back.

If the young blond god would only listen, as he stacked the pages back in their folder and picked up *Married* by Strindberg, *The American Boy's Handy Book*, and *Invertebrates of the Southern Hemisphere*.

"Son," he started.

"Son me again and I'll skin it," Billy hissed. He showed his fist. Then he took in the New York plates, the hair on the guy's chest that sprang out of his red-and-black checked lumber shirt like a mad dog, and the parrot's beak.

He called the station wagon a crap house, some kind of lending library, and Mort smiled.

Then Mort rolled the window down again and stuck his arm out to shake hands, but Billy was already folding his jacket and carefully laying it down on the lawn next to the girls' dining hall. A light went on upstairs in the infirmary. There was a flush. The light went out.

Mort went back to his books.

"Hey Jewboy," Billy called.

And that did it.

Billy tensed as the red and black shirt turned. His

ball-bearing ankles began to work. He hunched his shoulders forward and backward while the hairy head inside the car took off its extra eyes and set them carefully on the dash.

The good-looking broad in the Pontiac watched and Billy played to her; he splayed his nostrils and pawed the ground.

"Hey Jewboy," and he had himself a match. Nothing Billy loved more than hitting them where it hurt. He watched as the nearsighted mastodon got out, and was immediately surprised. An endless Jewboy with pig iron hands, tufted with Hebrew horsehair. A goddamn sonofabitchin' giant, for crissakes. . . .

Jewboy Dralon from Williamsburg, the Canarsie Kike. . . . It was going to be more kick than he thought, Big Billy Dawson from Lubbock.

Billy landed one first. While Mort was still getting out. While he was still comparing peaceful coexistence with the negative moral imperatives of . . .

A good one, high on the temple.

Mort's big hand went up and with it came a rush of old dog-eared memories.

Billy hit him again.

Something about a time when "Jewboy" was the only word in the dictionary. He wiped the second place where Billy hit him and his hand came away wet. Wet with more memories. He looked down at them. And another left. A winner, that left. Two more and another. Ashley watched Mort's head bob around on his neck, his body bob around on his legs. She wondered why he didn't hit back.

Mort remembered "Jewboy." It had been enough to get him to take off his glasses and move out of the car. And he remembered the other signals, too. The sensation of sticky wet on his fingers, the ringing from one ear to the other. He remembered a lot about the Canarsie Kike, but somehow he couldn't quite remember everything all at the same time. A lot of other ideas kept sneaking up on him. Syllogisms. A being unto B therefore compelling C and Camus's one who must stay, the long-ranged effects of the immediate solutions, ethics and cultures; all sorts of considerations beyond the Jewboy from Williamsburg.

The next hit brought him staggering to his knees. It was a long fall and jarred a lot of old memories. Hard ones. Memories of old streets and old pains. And Billy said, "Let's go, *Jewboy*," again and this time Mort remembered the key to the puzzle.

He reached up and grabbed Beautiful Big Billy by the shoulders. He closed his gorilla hands around those shoulders and squeezed. He felt the blond muscles rolling around on the bones. He squeezed some more. And Billy swung at him but couldn't get close enough. He could only graze the ends of Mort's checkerboard chest with the frantic grasp of a little kid.

It was way after two. The wind blew indifferently but still Mort couldn't actually hit back. Between memory and his fist were roller skates on dark stairs. It wasn't enough, the old street, and the chairs his mother used to splinter over his head. "Nervous idiot, the lummox," she used to call him.

But still he couldn't hit back.

And finally he couldn't even squeeze. He relaxed his fingers and opened his grasp. There was still time for questions and answers, he said . . . for does not the Jewboy cry out when he stubs his toe in the dark?

"Who gives a shit," Billy said. He turned away from the pain in his shoulders and without taking the time to shrug, threw himself into a right uppercut. And then a haymaker and a left cross. Ashley watched as Mort's grizzled profile rolled around like a discus, and then another left and two more rights.

Again and again and again, Billy kept hitting him and hitting him, but all Mort could feel was the weight of the old wooden chairs, the heft of his mother's curls done up in gilt like bonbons. He realized too that the hitting felt familiar. Warm and strangely protective. If he closed his eyes, he could almost touch her, his yellow-headed mama, in her flowered wrapper and the scuffs she'd made from his father's worn-out shlepping shoes.

Billy hit him some more and then Mort heard, "Daddy! Daddy?" And right away the feel of his mother's chintz slipped from between his grasp. . . . How would it look? His son should see gramma hit Daddy on the head with a chair? He turned towards Billy and gave him a couple of good feints, but it wasn't right. Man was still a time-binder. And what about Stonehenge? Ah Son, he said in silence, Man cannot live by fisticuffs alone. Without discovering the wheel we are as but the Anopheles mosquito. His palms turn upwards once more.

"For crissakes," Billy hissed. He spit in his face but

hit the next to the last red check before Mort's collar. Let's see the color of your right cross. Shit, it really chapped Billy's rear. He could see it, right in the center of Mort's eyes. . . . It goddamn didn't matter one fart *who* was down at the count. That big shit-assed, beaknosed, Jew York sonofabitch could turn the decision to win or lose, on and off like a radio knob. Winning didn't mean buggerall to the bastard and that reamed Billy's ass like nothing else, because Billy couldn't feature life amounting to a hell of a lot more, no matter what.

If winning wasn't the big apple, what the fuck was???? He closed his head against the answer. He didn't want to hear it. He could feel it come at him and come at him in waves from all directions. He wanted more than anything in the whole world to kill this bastard who could turn winning on and off like a radio.

"You Christ-killing, sheeny-fingered world-fucker!" Billy screamed. "They should have gassed your ass with the rest of . . ." But he never finished . . . this time there was no decision. The heck with Stonehenge, Mort lunged at him from the other end of mortality. Lunged for his neck with rabid fingers and wouldn't let go.

He choked him beyond choking, sat on his Aryan throat and squeezed out the sound of "Jewboy" until the cords buckled. Until the face went all black and phosphorescent. Until the blond body thrashed at the other end sidewards and sidewards, like dying fish and spastic dogs and puking colons and the finish of every-thing.

Rolling with him, down the sidewalk into the gutter under the Buick. Choking and choking him. Billy's eyes pumping in and out like a kid's birthday balloon. The American Bullfighter, *El Guero*, Navy Cadet Billy Dawson. BMOC, All-American End . . . Dying Billy . . . who had passed formation flying, carrier-landing, gunnery-training, night-flying, instrument-flying . . . dying under his Buick because Mort Dralon could turn winning on and off like a radio.

And Ashley ran out of the car and threw herself on her husband and pulled his hair and screamed at him and scratched and hollered in his ear and still he squeezed. And squeezed . . . until Rhile ran too and knelt by his head and said, "Why you kill him, Daddy?"

Only then did he let go . . . with a start. Only then did Billy Dawson fall to one side and lie there twitching. Eyes hanging there, half out of his head. Watching without seeing. Just enough breath left over to keep going with.

· 3 ·

afterwards was worse, this big Neanderthal down on his knees whimpering and slobbering over him like a sheepdog puppy with running eyes. Assuring him he abhorred violence, wringing his hands, outlining his philosophy of world brotherhood and the importance of unilateral disarmament for crissakes. It was all he could do to drag his burning body into his car and lock the doors. And still the fucker carried on. He didn't mean it. What the fuck, he didn't mean it. He almost tore his throat out, the sonofabitch, he didn't mean it.

For a long time he just leaned there and then watched as the goddamned goon got on his knees again, this time rocking the little boy and patiently explaining, as the kid tried to pull away from him, that violence was the last retreat of the anti-scientific or something. Through the rolled-up window, Billy wasn't sure.

He wanted the kid to realize that, he said four times; he said it over and over again as Billy managed to turn on the ignition and drive slowly around the corner and out of hearing. He watched the bigger man get on his feet, hand the boy back to his mother, and chase after him, to give him the name of his insurance company. He was screaming. In case, he said—in case there was anything he could do. Anytime, he was screaming, as Billy made it all the way to College Avenue.

He didn't know how he held himself together so long, but only when he could neither see nor hear the screwballed-up sonofabitch did he allow himself to collapse, to lean his throbbing skull against the steering wheel and let go. He sat there a long time just leaning his head and concentrating on breathing so it wouldn't hurt. In the rear-view mirror the Jew welts around his neck glowed Chinese red. He was drowning in thirst and sat there picturing the size of the glass. Deciding on a couple of quick Cours before he even thought about the first Four Roses. He ran his tongue over his cracked lip and only then found the energy to shift into second.

The Chuckwagon was closed and so was Lobo Eddies. Oh God, he wept, clutching the steering wheel as if it were Mort's neck, and thought about ROUND TWO and when and how he could set it up.

The half-lit glaze of the Orange Julius blinked a mute salmon on and off across his fingerprinted neck and Billy turned up Coal and rode past the tree streets, Elm, Hickory, and Hemlock, up through Yale, Columbia, Harvard, Dartmouth and into General MacArthur Road. He rested at the corner of Placitas and Colin P. Kelly and then turned back into Central where he headed past the first of the states . . . Montana, Louisiana . . . Dakota. The streets began to thin out past the fair grounds. There was a little taco joint where he knew he could wet his whistle and every couple of blocks, he'd slow to a crawl and practice moving his neck around so he wouldn't look like a stumblebum when he got there. Cocina de Blanca, he could see the sign up at the corner drawn by some near-sighted high school kid, the lettering so lousy you could hardly read it. And under the name the same kid had drawn a wet enchilada floundering in a glob of red chili. It was the only place open, so he pulled over to the curb and parked. Besides he knew the hungry pig would probably be the only one there.

For a long time he sat there with the motor running. His eye was swollen, he could feel it, and the pain of his neck was so strong he could barely swallow. Finally he turned off the motor and after a while, with a great burst of strength, got out of the car and leaned against the good fender, rolling his eyes back up under his forehead and then down again. He spit on a hanky and rubbed some of the defeat off his face, smoothed his hair, and began to walk towards the little cafe. He saw her through the window. She was sitting behind the counter, picking her nose. He stopped walking and watched as she rubbed the boogers under the counter. Behind her head were three Mexican ponchos on the walls, the crappy kind with the red, green, and yellow stripes that bled all over your hands before you even got them across the border, and just as she was about to stick her other thumb up her other nostril, he stepped into the room and her eyes loved him all over instead. He had two quick boilermakers and three long root beers, while she moved her lard ass around like a gyroscope. She asked him, "You O.K. Tex? Whatsa matter you no come in here now such a long time?"

He didn't answer her, so she started washing some glasses so she could still watch him, and after a while he told her how much he went for the ponchos on the walls. He needed something to get him to sleep and she would have to do. This is it, slit. . . . Nose-picking, sonofabitching, twat slit . . . this is it, so getyaself all ready, as she wiggled her leaking baby tits and a hundred-and-one bellies, and her smell like mildewed lard. Jesus, she was a pig. But it was late, and he knew he couldn't get to sleep with the smell of Jew all over him.

Come on, wetback, let's go, let's go get it over with.

She yakked all the way past the mesa towards 10, while his neck burned his guts, about, for godsakes, Lucy on TV and the craysee place she worked. The craysee people came in there, he wouldn't believe, and then more Lucy, out past the rockhound shop and the army surplus barn, like the time Lucy got her head caught in a loving cup, inching her sweaty thigh over on top of him, smelling like a ratty old pillow.

Did he see the one when Lucy worked in a chocolate factory? . . . and when she wiped her eyes, black lumps of mascara made stripes through her thick orange cheeks.

They drove through the crotch between the mountains and she had hold of his arm. She said her name was Rosemary Vigil and stared at the faint golden hairs that covered his hands like the damp mold on a flowerpot, the pulsing gooey wet already rising up from her, her breathing already thick and halting.

Behind them the city twinkled on and off like an old Lionel train and Billy was up to eighty, gas-pedaling the big Jew's eyeballs right through the floorboard.

"I can pass for Jewish," she said and he looked at her. "If I tell them my name is Cohen," she said, "or Greenberg or something."

"It's easy," she said. And then all of a sudden he laughed, reached over, and squeezed her knee until she yelled.

"Rosemary is my mother's name," he said. He let go.

"No kidding," she said. She looked at him, closed her eyes, and pretended again that it was she who had the yellow hair and the eyelashes that glowed around the eyes like daisy petals.

They drove beneath the overhanging trees and he slowed down. Up farther into the night pinion and juniper and then suddenly he stopped. He sat quietly for a long time listening to the motor die while Rosemary Vigil held her breath. She almost told him to hurry up but controlled herself. The palms of her hands were hot and sweaty and she rubbed them noiselessly against her skirts.

Billy sat for a long time trying to ease the soreness in his neck. The sharpness of the pain was gone, and if he didn't move, only the dull haze of a Dutch rub reminded him of ROUND ONE. He let the top of the convertible down and the sudden gush of pinion choked him. For the first time since he had run off to be a jet pilot, he realized he was back home.

She sighed and he forced himself to look at her, her mouth hanging open like a feeder in a gum machine. He bet her old man stuck his arm down toilets to make ends meet, a sleazy greaseball with a mustache that ran off the ends of his mouth like a rat's tail.

Fuck this Rosemary Vigil, who came to nookie point with her smell like a ratty old pillow. Whatever she got, she had it coming.

He turned towards her with his eyes closed, but her smell through his brain was a nail down a blackboard. Then hell, he jammed a hand down her blouse, grabbed her fat ass with the other one, and from then on it didn't matter what he did. His very touch set her into perpetual motion, a ten-finger push-pull toy that wrenched, jerked, pinched, grabbed, and took. The starving Armenian amok with a Hershey bar! She loved him and proved it by attacking him with open tit. Pushing them and twat, in and on him. Over and over, her fingers into his shirt, his ears . . . the mucus of one nostril and then the other . . . her blond American Tootsie Roll. Slobbering, and leaking all over his pants, disgusting him. And finally, because he expected it of himself, he turned to look at her and then forced himself to touch wet for wet, closing his eyes and trying not to smell; but it wasn't easy. It was very, very hard. She said, "In," but all he saw was "Exit" shining there in the dark like up in the balcony at the Gali Curci back home. "Exit" in red lightbulbs. But for her it was enough. She cried out like a small yellow dog used to the feel of cowboy boots in its slats, trembling under his unwilling hands, panting. She lay all curled up in a knotted heap like chicken's guts and then came without him. . . . Came one, two, ten times. Quickies, against his leg. With her fingers, beyond needing anybody. Which drew him further away. As she shuddered, he felt her vibrations rip through him. He pushed her off, pulled up his thighs, and felt his whole body stiffen, tighten, and finally turn to hot-cold lead weights. Then he turned towards her as she lay on her side all awry and unclean. He looked very fast, and then, even faster, pushed her. Hard. Till the side of her body hit the door handle and opened it. Then he reached into the back seat and threw her clothes out, out into the cold desert night on top of her—turned on the headlights and revved his motor.

"Hey!" she said, but Billy Dawson didn't hear "Hey!" He saw Jew and heard on and off, win-lose, like a million radio knobs. And he heard the sounds of decaying rooms falling in on him, and he chased her with his car. This spic whore, this cunt, who ran around in front of the car clutching her cheap satin brassiere in front of her belly button. He chased her and chased her, and if she hadn't fallen, at the last minute, into an arroyo, would have run her down, flattened her lard ass and her big boobs and finished her filthy screams and her spic moans one final time. He would have killed her and killed her and killed her till he couldn't kill her anymore.

· 4 ·

ASHLEY DRALON HATED IS-
rael, but Frijolito was worse. The landscape was bitter
and the town itself nothing but a couple of muddy
shells and a bar with swinging doors and a dirt floor.

The day after they moved in, the local school-bus
driver shot the father of two of his passengers in the bar
and two weeks later was back driving the bus. Everybody saw him pull out a gun, but good bus drivers
were hard to come by.

Mostly she hated the mud. Everything was choking
in it. And the loneliness. All day and night no one but
Rhile and Mort. Rarely she could see an occasional
woman shrouded in black *reboso* moving furtively from
one mud hut to another, but mostly not. She thought

desperately of how she had begged Mort to leave Israel and how she now found herself looking back nostalgically. Somewhere, she told herself, people lived differently, but no more was she really sure. More and more she felt like a parachute from a dandelion blown from one spot to another on indifferent winds.

Rhile played in the dirt as she moved from one pile of Mort's books to another with a dust rag. She stared into the mountains and thought about the hole in her life, the one that she couldn't quite put her finger on.

She thought about Mort. And knew she couldn't hate him. Mort just wasn't hateful. She sat on the edge of an unpacked box that said, "Clippings: *The London Economist* 1943–1947." She was sure she didn't hate him. Ashley didn't hate anybody. All she was sure about was wanting. That old hollow tunnel that stayed hungry no matter how many shells of sand she emptied into it.

At eleven, she had already become a master of not quite forgetting, not quite fingering whatever it was that dogged her. She sometimes, though, almost had a memory of the tall house with a park across the street. Of a girl in the dotted-Swiss pinafore that vaguely reminded her of the morning mirror. Tall white stockings to the knee? Did she? And a father who picked her up and breathed bourbon into her eyes? Did Ashley Tyler once have rooms and blocks and dolls that cried "Momma" when you pounded them from behind? Well, maybe. It was possible. If only she could sit long enough. With her eyes closed tightly enough.

Ashley-Not-Quite. Everybody had always said it was a shame she hadn't inherited at least some of the old girl's you-know. She supposed it was, but really Mother was just another fuzzy house in her mind. A distant, not quite real image that pounded in between her memories like a stitch in the side. Even at her age, everybody said, Thalia Tyler Clukis was an act Poor-Old-Ashley'd never even begin to follow, as she followed her, and followed her, from one country to another, game to another, act to another, all her life.

She'd once read in *The Ladies' Home Reader* that a child might develop personality difficulties if left too often alone and so Ashley prided herself on being home with her child. It proved she was a good mother. She rubbed her swollen belly and dusted Mort's *New Cyclopedia of Practical Quotations*. It was still early and Rhile messed with the sand in front of the door. Really he was watching Mommy, a dust cloth statue through the window, but Mommy was looking further than Rhile. It was enough Mommy was home. Mommy was watching the world because she measured her life not in *coffee spoons* but window frames.

Maybe she should start supper. The beans always took so long to cook. Mort had told her it was the altitude. Maybe the crying was, too. And maybe she should write to Thalia. Mothers knew best. She thought about taking Spanish at the university, it was only sixty miles. Or English. Reading was good for you. Was Rhile calling? She wondered what he wanted. She picked up a few pieces of wood for the stove. It sounded like he was crying.

"What's wrong, Rhile?" she said and looked beyond him to the vast emptiness that seemed to follow her.

One empty place was connected to another. And another, dating back again to that dotted-Swiss pinafore. Or had it only been a picture she'd seen once in somebody else's family album? They didn't have a family album. Or a house anyplace, or a park, or what? What was it you were supposed to have that she didn't? The child filtered through again only on the back-up from the muted time when she was just like anybody. She remembered the school named after a saint.

"For gawdsakes, Hillary," her mother used to say. (It used to bother her that Hillary was her father's name. But that was then—when someone named He had a golden smile through the golden glass in the golden time when she was sure she'd had one. That dotted-Swiss pinafore in bumpy blue, if not yellow. When Hillary was still around and schools started at one particular time and ended at another.) Oh God, everything was so jumbled. She was crying again. And wringing the dust rag over *The Romance of Leonardo da Vinci*. She picked it up and thumbed through it from page vii to the translator's notes, page 637.

When she went to the school—named after the saint, she wore a blue plaid uniform and was at the age when being eleven years old exactly meant going on twelve. "What's wrong?" she called to her son through the windowpane. They did a lot of skiing at the school, going up and down the hills all the days, all the nights. Ashley too. She was a good skier. She played tennis. She rode like Dale Evans and her French was as good as her Portuguese, Spanish, and Italian, but the time she was thinking back to, she wasn't . . . skiing. She could hear the boy say something to her, but he was so far away. She was only just going on twelve and in the distance just behind him, she could see them skiing up and down. She was sitting alone with her poles stuck into the snow behind her, and her skis. She'd gone back over to the quads and sat outside shivering. She was sick.

Over and over the little boy kept telling her something, but she only just shook her head. She wanted to throw up. How could he tell her now. She was home. She was a good mother, only not now . . . now she was trying to remember what besides food you could throw up. What, all over the ski slopes? Nauseous, still as death, afraid to go in, unable to go back for her things. She half-remembered the Jack London story about the man who froze to death because his hands were too cold to strike a match and she shook her head. No, that wasn't what she was trying to remember, and the little boy pulled at her, kicked her and beat his red fists on her knees. "It's cold," the little boy cried. The little boy was her son. His name was Rhile.

Yes, she was cold. She remembered, and when she couldn't stand it anymore, she had leaned against a tree, but the little boy didn't care. He wanted his mother and there she was, but still she wouldn't come home. No, she said. No, let me remember how hard it had been to walk. How I had to concentrate. First one foot and then the other. My legs, rusted and brittle underneath me. How I used to take communion with my innocent eyes, all the time hiding the true me. The sin inside where it didn't show. Pretty maids all in a row. It was all framed in her mind like petrified wood samples, how she had made herself kneel so that God in his Episcopal Heaven wouldn't make a special trip down to wreak his vengeance on her.

Then, all the time then, so much finer than the little boy telling her about now. And then somewhere in that void between then and now she was aware that the little boy's wrists were frozen. That he wanted to make. She thought she closed the door, but couldn't quite make out if that left him in or out.

She realized she was bleeding. She knew everything was lost. Either way, she would pay. From God or the god of the quad, Ursula Herter; that she remembered clearly—so she stayed on in the chapel. Hoping God's way would be first . . . knocking her over with one clean, all-forgiving blow. If she went back to the quad, Ursula would be there. She was always there and would find out. She would extract her own payments . . . poke, pull off the sheets. Hold her legs apart and stick up fingers. Ursula would know.

She begged for death as the last of the day slipped down behind the mountains.

But of course it was Ursula. It was always Ursula, and the others, wherever she ran to hide. Then, and now too. Ursula, who insisted that everybody line up just before *lights-out* down in the washroom. Made them, one by one, raise their naked arms and lower their cotton underpants. Ursula, who searched mercilessly for one lone hair either place. Ursula, who forced the nightly prayers from each of them. The prayer that they not, *ever ever ever*, be the first to sin. And here it was, the ultimate, worse than an entire bushful of wild hairs; the disgusting, youth-denying blood loss. She was a woman and there was no turning back. She waited and waited, but God did not appear. And finally she had no one to turn to but Ursula.

And it was just the way she had lived it in the chapel. It *was* Ursula who tore into her, like a frog on a biology table. Who pointed her finger and called her their wild cell. Who insisted she forfeit all rights to childhood thereafter. Who forced her into the midnight purgatory of the washroom with nothing but her bloody evidence to huddle against till Madame found her lying in a pool of horror and hysteria.

A stiff core of pain up through the blood to her heart, where it lay and even still crouched. She could, even through her old terror, feel the motion of her legs pulling against one another. As they'd pulled then. In a useless gesture of holding in what poured out to damn her forever.

"Momma," the little boy screamed. "Momma," over and over until she had to hear.

"Why do you stay out in the cold until you make in your pants?" she asked him as the distance shifted and the snow turned to mud. She took a course once and read that the preschool child had a difficult time relating his exterior world to his needs. She took off her son's pants.

She wondered if the beans were done yet. And what had ever happened to Ursula Herter and when Mort would be home. Maybe she should take Spanish at the university, or English.

· 5 ·

THE FIRST TIME TRINIDAD
Lucero had stood in front of an audience up on a stage
was back at Alameda High School, at the Forensic Society's big Socrates debate.

Socrates: Past and Future
Socrates: Live or Die?

Trini had been assigned to debate the offensive
viewpoint, that Socrates, in his role as moral conscience-
pricker had disrupted the flow of community life and
should therefore be punished.

"Dissension is always the enemy of civilization!" he
had said. He had banged his left fist into his right palm

and followed up with: "Society has no choice . . . it must, to preserve itself, silence the dissenter for his own good." This sentiment he had illustrated by raising his palms upward, which, according to *The Beginner's Guide to Public Speaking*, best illustrated the mood called spiritual supplication. The audience had loved him. They sentenced Socrates to death, and Trini had been awarded the F for Forensics for his school sweater. That moment had stood in Trini's memory as the high point of his entire life.

Now Trinidad Lucero stood before judge and jury for the second time. But this time he, not Socrates, was on trial, and the only letter he would be awarded was a big C for Communist. The episode did have a certain irony though, for this time, like the first, Trini would vote with the side of the majority decision. If the Board of Education found him guilty, who was he to argue? No less than Socrates . . . he, too, was happy to accommodate himself, and was more than willing to take his hemlock.

Dave Collins, the Legislative Guild Representative, kept his eye only surreptitiously on the teacher of band instruments as the charges were leveled. The entire proceedings took less than an hour. They convened at twelve and by a quarter of one, the board had already ripped off Trini's conductor's epaulets and cracked his baton over their knees. Trini's eyes were moist, but he knew he deserved it. He, like his predecessor, had only gotten what they deserved; the only difference between them was that he hadn't meant to disrupt, not even a little bit.

But still the Board of Education found Trinidad Lucero a threat to the youth of the community. They also found it incumbent upon themselves to relieve him immediately of all further responsibilities. Dave Collins made sure everybody saw him nod vigorous approval at the decision and Trini Lucero shook his head back and forth and went "tsk tsk" silently with his tongue.

The Second Undersecretary of Proceedings had accused Trini of being sole arbiter of what the Tiheras Valley Junior High School Marching Band did and did not play at the half times of their football engagements.

The First Oversecretary of Intercommunications said that therefore he and he alone was solely responsible for the subversive nature of his selections.

The teacher of band instruments himself stood under the glare of blinding spotlights and had to agree with them, and the rope of circumstantially incriminating evidence tightened.

It did not, the Assistant Principal said, matter, in these troubled times, what the tonal values of Rimski-Sakorsky amounted to. How did it look for an American football team to spin its baton to the Russian's common time. Plus which, the Constituent Spokesman in charge of Further Enrollment testified that the Board had had their eyes on Trinidad Lucero long before Lieutenant Kijé. Did the other members of the committee realize that of all the teachers in the entire district, it was this Trinidad Lucero who had been the very first to sign the statewide loyalty oath?

A general hush fell over the assembled committee. The eyes of the Legislative Guild Representative rolled twice into his head and then back before roosting. Heads shook and mouths worked. The loyalty oath signing would prove to be the clincher, for, as the Undersecretary of the Second Sons of Liberty would point out, what did lying under oath mean to a Communist? "First?" he said. "Why first, unless you were planning, from the start, to pull the wool over America's innocence?"

The Undersecretary's deep baritone voice, massaged just five minutes before with an index finger full of vaseline, was so deep, so heartfelt, and so resonant, that he brought tears to everybody's eyes, especially Trini's, who would, at that moment, have cut off his balls to defend the state's right to step on his neck. He deserved it, he told himself, him and Socrates. . . . Who did they think they were?

The case was really a shoo-in when the Board brought their star witness. His name was Henry Koehler and he played second-chair trombone in the second-string band. Henry Koehler's evidence was as good as a signed confession, for he said, in his childish, half-changing voice, that this same Trinidad Lucero had once told the entire ninth grade that in his opinion Paul Robeson had a very nice voice.

Well . . . *The Daily Herald* called Trini a Communist cancer-carrier. The entire story was right out there on page one. Not only had this cunning beast forced their innocent children to listen to *Scheherazade* but had them playing, not only Kijé at their football games, but what about *The Red Poppy* ballet, which was practically the "Indian Love Call" for the Russian navy?

"*Hijo de Dios*," Trini moaned when he realized what he had done. "Firing is too good for me. My father, Dr. Ysofio Lucero-Casadas, was right. I am a discredit to my family, a blight on my race, a disgrace to the Holy Mother Church. And just imagine what they'd say if they knew I'd also played *America* by Charles Ives, mauled and variationed out of all recognition. The only course left to me now is to make an example of myself for posterity, lay my sedition on the line for all to spit upon, and take the cuts and bruises such infamous behavior deserves . . . so that others might profit by my suffering example."

· 6 ·

ASHLEY LOOKED OUT THE window and watched Mort coming with his head down inside the paper. It was a local weekly and she was in for it. Just like last week he'd talk all night, all during dinner, while she was fixing it, while she cleaned up afterwards. He'd tell her every single thing in the whole paper including the Help Wanted and then what he thought it really meant and what they ought to do to change things, for instance that music teacher, that Mexican, the one they fired for Communistic leanings. How did Mort know for sure he wasn't a threat to the nation's security—how did he know? For heaven's sake if a man didn't even know how old he was, how was he so cocksure about everybody else in the world. She counted silently with her fingers and figured. Let's see, I met him in forty-eight, we were married next . . . and he was how old, sure, he was . . . which made him. . . . She was positive. Mort was only thirty, no matter what he thought. And that's what she meant about this Trinidad Lucero, the music teacher.

"Well, don't you think a band leader ought to have the right to pick out whatever song he pleases?" he'd asked her. "I tell you our very liberties are at stake."

"Catsup or relish?" she asked him.

"And don't think his being Mexican did him any good either."

"Succotash?"

"He probably had to beg on the streets when he was a kid. You remember those urchins, the calluses on their heels thick as pig skin?"

"You see son," he said to the boy—"a man must fight for what he believes in." He drew his chair closer and showed him Trinidad Lucero's picture. "You see this man?" The boy saw. "This man lost his job. It's time the boy had his first practical lesson in the responsibilities of a citizen in a democracy," he said to his wife.

"Let him eat his succotash." Ashley picked up Rhile's plate and tipped it so the water from the vegetables didn't touch his meat. If they touched he wouldn't eat either one.

"This is important, Ashley. We are living through another Spanish Inquisition, all you have to do is read the papers, the boy must learn who his enemies are."

"Don't pick at your food," Ashley said. "Eat it before it gets cold."

"He's lucky they didn't blind him when he was a kid."

"Who?" Rhile asked.

"The man, honey. The man they fired."

"Why did they blind him?"

"They didn't," Mort said. "Daddy said he's lucky because they didn't. Never mind Rhiley, one day Daddy will take you down into Mexico and show you the poor starving children and the suffering masses and the unfortunates huddling together in boxcars with nothing to burn to keep them warm, and nothing to wrap their feet in and . . ."

"Do you want Mommy to butter your bread for you, Rhiley?"

"Sure, *he* has bread, but what about this poor Lucero fellow? What will *his* children eat? I tell you it's criminal, firing a man for choosing a melody of his own choice to play with his own orchestra."

"Band, I thought you said it was a band?"

"What's the difference? Does it make the man a Communist?"

· 7 ·

THE KID IN THE ORANGE SKI
sweater wasn't as young as he looked. With some people, what they go through in life is all over their faces;
with others, it's Dorian Gray all over again.

He waited for the two faggots to leave for the movies and then got in through their kitchen screen. For a
week now he'd been using their place to shower in.
They went out a lot and he was used to being careful.
The *Herald* was open to the movie sheet and *Captain
from Castille* with *Body and Soul* were circled with red
pencil. Even if they just stayed for only one—either
Tyrone Power or John Garfield—that gave him, he
figured, at least three hours, but he was pretty sure
those two would make them both.

· 42 ·

First he sat on the couch and relaxed. It had been quite a week. The best in his life, if you figured that nobody, no matter what he did, would ever find out and punish him. He took off the sweater and carefully set it over the arm of the couch. Having left home quickly, he hadn't gotten away with much. He sat back. That was when he saw the poster. SAVE LUCERO it said, on two hand-lettered lines. Jack thought it would have looked better if it had all been on one. More dramatic. His pants he lay on the other arm. Then he took off his socks and his shorts and walked into the bathroom. He was thinking about all the women he'd done it to that week. And about the car accident and the fight with the blond wide receiver and the enormous gorilla. He stopped to do four knee bends and one push-up. In all ways it had been a terrific idea, running away from home, and finally doing what *he* wanted to do. But he had to get into the shower now, first things first.

The reason he always took a shower right after having a woman was only common sense and the reason he never made the mistake of taking a bath was that even well-scrubbed tubs left films of undetected germs. He laughed, thinking of the expression on the gorilla's face when he'd first seen him pulling on the so-called rope. Like he might have had a heart attack. Well, you couldn't have everything. Jack had long since learned that. The accident itself was pretty good and he'd have to be satisfied. The water was hot and for a long time he stood with the spray on his back. Then he started with his neck and worked down his body with his own natural sponges and Lifebuoy soap, shuddering as he kicked Lester's washcloth out of his way. He didn't know it was Lester's. All he knew was that it belonged to one of the fags and that they wouldn't be back until eleven.

He scrubbed his body very slowly and carefully. Behind his ears, down his arms, underneath and through his hair, missing nothing. Especially around the balls. There three times. Poking gently and meticulously inside the head.

Sex was a purgative, that he knew, but the female was basically filthy. Her dank hole packed with a swampy mucus was never totally cleansed, which was why it was so important for them to douche regularly, but he knew they didn't. . . . None of them.

He soaped his sponge for the second go-round and this time rubbed so hard the top layer of bright red capillaries burst, leaving bleeding red welts all over and especially from his lower belly down to the middle of his thighs. It was all part of his obligation to himself, the price he was willing to pay for his indulgences. If only *they* would do likewise. . . . Morning, night, and immediately afterwards. A strong solution of vinegar and distilled water in a douche bag. He shuddered and let the hot spray from the shower nozzle burn his head. Then he shut off the water, got the Mercurochrome from the medicine chest, and doused himself liberally all around his cock. Then he lay down on the cool tile floor and pulled and pulled until the final cleansing spurt came all over his leg.

Jack had run away from his father, Martin W.

Samuels, without leaving a note, but he did leave messages. He laughed again, got up, and got dressed. He was told once by a fortune-teller that he had a license to sin, because of his clean unblemished palm, and so he supposed he was entitled. Not that he considered his little escapades sins exactly. This time he laughed quite loud. He doubted whether Martin W. Samuels would have agreed with either the fortune-teller or him.

If it hadn't been too risky, Jack would have thought of registering at the university, but he was sure his father was sparing no expense in his frantic effort to locate him, so he settled for sneaking in and out of the apartment and sometimes the men's dorm for showers. He'd already gotten a job driving a milk truck for Valley Gold, and was pretty sure he'd get himself a place to stay just like anybody else.

Staying by himself was a brand new experience for Jack. He'd spent eight years at the Menninger Clinic, where they were always watching you, and later, at Austen Riggs. That was after he'd put on sixty pounds on insulin therapy, not that it showed now. Now he was tall, dark, and handsome, with, people said, a magnetic pull in the center of his eyes. Not that he'd been exposed to that many people, plain street people, outside one institution or another or his family. But then there was that license. And it was the license Jack felt he was exercising when he left home. If not to sin, then surely to expand. He picked up his father's cat by the scruff of its neck. Expanding under the full scrutiny of his father was ridiculous, look at his mother, three-foot-nothing and shrinking every year. He'd long ago decided that when he left he'd let kitty leave his dad the message.

Her name was Angela, his father's cat, had six toes and was whimpering as she lay in her box with her legs rubber-banded together. She alternated whimpering with a spitting hissing and a frantic thrashing, but Jack had tripled the rubber bands. The red kind that Andy Boy broccoli came tied together with and his father never threw out. The cat whipped her body back and forth trying to get out of her shit. Cats hate shit. It's like wet wool to them, shit. But Jack already had the tape recorder set up, and only wished he'd had a movie camera.

Martin W. had gotten the cat as a small kitten one summer on a family outing to Deer Isle, and the first night the fuzzy bundle had slept in the house, she had leaped on his father's pajama leg in the middle of the night when the industrial tycoon was on his way to the crapper. She had dug her baby claws in, all of them, and his father had found her adorable. Jack never remembered his father finding anything or anybody adorable in his whole life, ever.

Jack had already folded the bedclothes and moved his books and papers off the desk, storing everything that wasn't going in his closet. Nothing was left out because one couldn't be too careful when it came to science.

Pussy seemed to know she had been naughty and Jack duly recorded same into the tape. In an experiment such as this everything had to be meticulously annotated. He recorded her furtive glances and her frantic movements and made particular note of the desperate way she tried to free her freak paws from their strangling bonds.

Then Jack described his desk. The bottle of cleaning fluid, pitcher of water, and safety matches. The bottle of formaldehyde borrowed from the local high school's biology lab. The bottle with the mouse in several severed pieces, a tooth hanging on the end of a long string of palate tissue.

He had already sealed the windows and the door with felt insulating strips in case his father returned early, which he doubted, because Martin W. usually accomplished what Martin W. set out to accomplish, and this particular evening had been dedicated to a fine dinner, an evening at the theater, and perhaps a nightcap afterwards. He had taken his wife, Jack's mother, with him.

Jack described his own heavy breathing into the tape recorder, and the sweat that poured off him. He said he could feel a definite increase in the flow of adrenalin but that his hands were steady and his pulse regular.

Then, when everything was quite ready, he sat in the moiré armchair by the window, between the cat in its shit box and the desk with the necessary ingredients. From there he read into the tape recorder, over the frantic howling of the cat, the generic description of both victim: *Mus musculus*, whose tail was scaly and hairless in some parts, hairy in others (now deceased) ; and assailant, a small domestic carnivorous mammal, related to the lion, tiger, leopard, jaguar, and puma, *Felis libyca domestica*.

He described *Felis libyca domestica*'s game with *Mus musculus*. How it had first cornered it in the pantry, darted, feinted, and secured it between freezer and dryer. How pussy stuck confident, misshapen claws into its victim's flesh a bit at a time, letting it run itself exhausted between one machine and the next, while all the time prescribing its area little by little. He told how the cat very slowly pawed the mouse to shreds, nipping a bit here, jabbing at it there. And he described in rather great detail the terrified panic of the mouse. He spent almost fifteen minutes telling that part.

Jack Samuels lifted his legs up on the end of his bed and told how *Mus musculus* dragged its bleeding carcass from one illusory haven to the next, bits of sticky hair falling out over all of the basement, and how it got ground into the Spanish tiles his father had ordered all the way from Barcelona. He reported that the cat leaped and pounced on the mouse the same way it pounced on the bits of fluff under his bed and how pussy seemed to enjoy its victim's death throes. Then, just before he turned off the recorder so he could get a Coke, he told how *Felis libyca domestica* presented his father with *Mus musculus*'s bloody carcass as a gift and how Martin W. gave to the cat a warm glass of cream, took her into his lap, and scratched her behind the ears for exactly thirteen minutes nonstop.

With the Coke, Jack ate four fig newtons. Then he carried the tape recorder into his bathroom and placed it on the lid of the toilet seat. He went back for the cat box, and holding it as far away from his own body as possible, he set it and *Felis libyca domestica* into the bathtub, telling her all the while that what was to happen now was just one more proof of the inextricable chain of protoplasmic continuity.

As he poured the cleaning fluid over the cat's fur he catalogued each of her movements into the recorder, then he sat on the tile floor and recorded her screams of anguish as he set the match to her. Her thrashing became wild, she flipped herself back and forth from the box into the tub and there from side to side . . . howling and screaming. Jack described each of her movements as vividly as possible so as to have a precisely accurate record.

Unfortunately the experiment's continuity was finally ruined when the flames reached the rubber bands and the cat was able to run. She then leaped, Jack said, like Halley's Comet, out of the tub and through the tiny room, knocking over the recorder and disconnecting the microphone. But it was worth it, he described later, because, as she darted out, the wind fired the flames and the spectacle was absolutely breathtaking.

After his shower, Jack looked around the purloined apartment. From the looks of the medicine chest one of the fags had an ulcer. They had quite a collection of Indian rugs, neat underwear drawers, and three jars of vaseline, one of them in the refrigerator. A back room was loaded with dusty old portfolios, and opening them, Jack found pictures of Old Soldier's Homes in charcoal and smudged wash, modernistic men in overalls waving colored fists at God and red, yellow and blue still lifes chinked together with bits of ripped newspaper. Whoever was the art student was strictly no talent as far as he could make out and judging by his SAVE LUCERO posters all over the joint, he couldn't letter either.

Having just come to town Jack didn't recognize the name Lucero but he did print DON'T in front of SAVE on three of them. Then he fixed himself a malted, washed out the blender, took a couple of apples and climbed up on the flat roof where he'd already stashed his father's best quilt and insulated, rubber-lined duck-hunting jacket.

· 8 ·

IT WAS LATE WHEN RON Harkness and Lester Newbauer got back from *Captain from Castille*. All the way home they argued about who liked who better, Power or Garfield, but the real gist of their anger was Lester's posters.

"This is no time to play Patrick Henry," Ron screamed at him. "I tell you they're firing garbage collectors for subversive activities."

"Look, Harkness," Lester said, "nobody's going to tell me who to feel for."

"Feel? You want to feel the FBI up your ass?"

"Whose house is it anyway?" Lester screamed, and instead of just turning the damn posters in for Lettering and Illumination 310, he ran out of the house and tacked them up in The Pig's Eye, the Library, and the Student Union.

Nobody was going to talk to Lester Newbauer that way. Especially since he'd once gone to a rally. Back in Chester, Pa., to save the Sacco Boys, or had it been Scottsboro and Vanzetti, it was so long ago he couldn't remember anymore, but it gave him clout anyway. Lester Newbauer was socially conscious if nothing else, and the more hysterical Ron got, the more he was willing to risk for the shnook band leader who'd gotten himself sacked for playing the wrong 4/4 at the wrong time.

"For godsakes," he said to Ron, who slammed out the door threatening to screw his cock right down to the roots. . . . "When they interviewed the jerk on WQED, he said the Board of Education knows best." "You're exaggerating," screamed Lester, waking Jack Samuels, who'd been fast asleep on the roof. "The poor bastard doesn't have enough sense to . . ." but Ron was gone. "It's ridiculous," he muttered to himself. "Like living with a booby trap, set to spring on the spur of . . . goddammit," he screamed, stubbing his toe, "it's a question of public spirit," but in his heart of hearts he knew his lover was right. Jack didn't care one way or the other, at that hour he just wished his adopted neighbor-landlords would shut the hell up.

Lester was the one with the ulcer. And the art student. Actually it wasn't quite clear whether he was in art or art ed. After eleven undergraduate years even his guidance counselor had lost track, but after TB, diabetes, nephritis, ulcers, a dislocated spine, and his less dramatic disabilities neither the Scholarship Committee nor either department was pressuring him, so Lester just took a little Lettering and Illumination here and a little Educational Psychology someplace else and lived the student's life down to a science.

Before Ronald Harkness, Ph.D., came West to be with Lester, things had been different. Perhaps, Lester thought, pouring himself a little half-and-half, he might have made a homecoming poster instead of one crying for social justice if things had stayed the way they had been. But now, much as he loved Ron, and he loved him, yes, he did, he absolutely loved and adored him, he always seemed to be proving something to himself.

The night Ron arrived, Lester'd been out taking a walk over to the Methodist church with the dog. It was a small dachshund named Fritzie Katzenjammer that two days later ran away. The thought had once occurred to him that the dog hadn't run away, that something sinister had happened to him, but Ron, who was a psychologist and ought to know, had told him that was defensive, paranoic, and psychologically ungrounded. He remembered turning, after Fritzie had done his business and seeing a light on in the apartment and he also remembered wondering who it was. Then he didn't remember anything. Only Ron. Ron reading *The Arizona Highways*, Ron wearing *his* terrycloth bathrobe. Ron clucking Fritzie under his chin and then dropping him on his short legs like a cat.

Lester was freckled rosy and chunky, with leftover broken pieces of him stuck together into places they were never quite happy with. He had a peculiar cackling laugh which rose from his off-center trunk like spastic hiccups and he could hear himself laughing when the dog fell. He could still remember the odd sound of his own laugh, of the sense of himself listening to it, and of the moaning in the dog's cry.

"Not that way, silly," he'd said to Ron, catching up the little animal and loving it. "That's no way to treat man's best friend." But still he'd laughed and he remembered it.

"Aren't you going to say hello?" Ron said, smiling at him in that Tallulah way of his as the magazine slid to the floor. He became aware of his own odor coming from Ron's body and it added to his nervousness. He sensed himself shifting his weight from one unbalanced hip to the other as he watched Ron get up, pass the coffee table and come nearer. Ron had his arms out and kicked at the dog imperceptibly as he came.

It had taken Lester a lot longer to adjust to the idea of Ron than to Ron himself. He'd always had a girlfriend. He'd always known one day he'd marry her. Her name was Joyce and it comforted him to know that even though she lived far away, she lived. And then there was Ron, "That makes me, that makes me not," and Joyce, his long-time affidavit of heterosexuality drifted out to sea.

Lester needed a Gelusil. Just thinking about the first time Lester Newbauer with varicose veins became Ron Harkness's concubine in chinos. He could almost see Joyce's name tattooed on his dick sink into the foreskin. Then he needed a phenol washed down with half-and-half.

"Shit," Lester said to himself as he realized Ron wasn't coming back right away. "Shit on a brick," as he looked at his watch and also realized it was too late to go to The Pig's Eye to take down his SAVE LUCERO poster. The truth was they *were* firing garbage collectors for subversive activities. And what, really, did he care what the Board of Education thought should be played or not played at half time at a high school football game? Ron, as usual, was right. He poured himself a glass of milk, then warmed it, added a little honey, and hummed "Danny Boy." Still Ron didn't show. He went to bed. He set the clock for seven and hoped he got to the library, the SUB, and the Pig before the FBI.

SAVE LUCERO, his crawnce. . . . Screw Lucero, more like it.

· 9 ·

ASHLEY LAY SHIVERING IN
her flannel nightgown trying hard to fall asleep before
Mort was through bathing the boy. The sounds of her
husband's English soap fleet going down to defeat at
the hands of her son's Israeli sponges played around
through her mind like a recurring nightmare.

Then she tried not to hear the story of the Balfour
Declaration as Rhile stood on the toilet seat and Mort
wiped him dry with the big striped towel. Each crevice,
each spot. His long fuzzy arms. His elbows, already
square and jutting. Then the tales of the Hagannah
heroism as Daddy "flew" him down the dark hall to his
bed and tucked him in. She had said she had a headache. She tried to block their sounds out. She tried to

still her breathing. She tried to fall asleep faster than she could fall.

When she stuck out just a little further, she'd tell him the doctor said it was no good for the baby.

In the morning, Mort said, they were driving into Duke City. She stiffened when the boy called goodnight to her.

He'd wonder if she didn't answer him.

She'd have no excuse if she did.

"Goodnight, Mommy," he called again, and it was little enough. . . .

"Goodnight, Rhile," she called.

She lay back and let her eyes fall open wide.

She heard her son's door close. She heard him say he wanted a drink of water. She heard Mort go to the bathroom, fill up a cup, and bring it to him. She heard Mort say, "Sleep tight, son." She heard the door open and close twice more and then she heard the sounds of his feet down the hall.

The covers were pulled tightly and the lights off when he came in, but he sat heavily on the end of the bed and said, "Lee?" shaking her hip with a handful of heavy fingers. When she didn't answer he turned on the light and then, remembering that she couldn't stand it with the light on, turned if off again.

He was cold. His thick toenails scratching her bare legs as he slid into bed left a flaky trail of dead skin. She turned around as he covered her with itch and found his black eyes sucking her blood. Over his shoulder, out in the hall, she could see a few darker stripes against the wall, shadows from the slats of the kitchen chair in the light from the bathroom. Boxes and slats, slats and boxes. She focused on the image of the treble clef from the shadow of the chair on the wall. She remembered when she took piano.

She was on her back and he laid his head on her belly and listened to the sounds of his seed. He had her nightgown already bunched up under her armpits. He moved around and the thick matted hair from his chest dragged behind him like a clubfoot.

She was cold. He hurt, scratching and itching. Mashing her body into red grits. She propped herself up on one elbow as he fooled around with her porcupine. His little porcupine, he said.

"Don't forget the kidneys," she said. "And pinto beans, when you go into town tomorrow, and also some liver if he has any fresh."

He grunted.

"Or if he doesn't have liver, get some bones; neck or marrow, it doesn't matter which."

"O.K.," he said, kissing. Her bosoms. Her flattish, triangular bosoms with their albino-centered eyes peering up into his molars. Every so often he'd reach down to see if she was ready. Then he rolled her over, which irritated her because she was right in the middle and had to start all over again.

Matches. Oil. Celery. Onions.

It wasn't easy getting a whole week's grocery list ready in the dark, without a pencil or anything.

He was pumping and pushing, harder and harder, until he lay flat and heavy.

"Finished?" she said. "Can I cover up now," she asked. "I'm freezing."

For a minute he just lay there. Then all of a sudden, fell off her in one heavy heap.

"Did you set the clock?" she asked, and he either muttered yes or no and then started in twitching. Each muscle jerking to another rhythm, arms, legs, neck, the whole wilting body.

She shrugged, pulled the covers back up, fixed her nightgown, and shut her eyes. If he didn't care if the clock was set, why the heck should she?

But this time Mort wasn't asleep for good. After a while he jerked awake with a start and for the next hour lay there staring at the ceiling and deciding what could be done for the unfortunate music teacher. The man's fate was on Mort's conscience. After all, he was a fellow sufferer. And they were, all of them, in this world together, with the same problems, the same desires . . . the same.

"Turn over, Mort, you're snoring."

"How can I be snoring? I'm not even . . ." but he turned over anyway, it was easier than trying to explain to her the weight of his responsibilities . . . the burden of his awareness. . . .

· 10 ·

and one thirty in the morning Lester Newbauer was
aware that he was no longer alone. He clutched at his
throat and was sure that all was over, he had been
apprehended. Then a familiar voice asked him what a
Lucero was and why it was up to them to save it. It
called him "ole buddy" and scared him. That particular
voice didn't say "ole buddy" without some good reason,
so Lester rubbed his tongue over the plush on his teeth
and opened his eyes. It was too early. He couldn't have
been responsible for garbage collectors and posters yet.
"Ole buddy" spelled Billy Dawson, in, he could see, a
blue turtleneck and white ducks. He caressed his own
tongue. Billy had always put the fear of God and the

desire for false idols into his soul with the same blow. Oh blow, blow.

"Come on there, Newy. What the hell's a Lucero?"

Lester lay there still. The first word would settle everything. Would lay him open for the NKVD or let him rescue everything. He had to be careful. Billy Dawson could pounce on your insufficiency like a puppy on a dirty sock.

"The wing-beaked Lucero, you ignoramus."

He rolled over and rubbed his eyes.

"Rare, Dawson, very rare."

"No shit," Billy said, with that little smile of his. "The wing-beaked Lucero eh? Well, can't seem to find my Audubon Society bird book, there, Newbauer. . . . Kind of sets me back," he said, watching him.

Lester sat up. He watched him back.

"Hell, Dawson, I didn't think bird watching was up your alley. Whatever happened to the navy?" All the time figuring: Why he'd come? What was the angle?

He propped another pillow under him and watched Billy pick at his teeth with the side of a matchbook cover, walk to Lester's dresser, and run his finger across the top of it.

"I told you I'd be back in time for late registration," Billy said. He looked at his finger and held it up to the light.

"Inspection perfect. . . ." He shook his head. "What happened? Your old man finally croak and will you the family nigger?" Which was Billy's way of letting Lester know he knew all about Ron Harkness even if he had been away.

"Who're you shitting, Dawson?" He rubbed his sleep-grained eyes. "In and out just like that? Last time I heard, you were off to Pensacola to join the Navy Cadets. Bad heart or something?"

"Bad nothin'. It's over, that's all. I went. I got what I was after and I'm back."

"Just like that?"

"Brains, Newbauer. . . . All it takes is brains. How to con the army *and* the navy out of your ass by Billy Dawson . . . want a copy?" Shit no, he thought contemptuously, they didn't draft faggots . . . Billy spit a little air on his nails and rubbed them on his pants.

"Then how?"

"I'll tell you about it some time, when we've got a couple of days."

Lester was getting more nervous. Billy gave him a watch-out look and started walking around the room looking at everything. Picking up a hairbrush, kicking at a dropped shoe. . . .

"That's easy," Lester said, suddenly trying a long shot. "For you, I've got a couple of weeks." He reached for Billy's arm and pulled him to the side of the bed. "What's the matter, you seem jumpy."

Billy pulled away and then, so he wouldn't look either suspicious or defensive, sat down real casual by the foot and leaned up against the iron railing. Lester smiled.

It was a long shot all right, but what the hell, he noticed that Big Billy was making no move to get up from the foot of the bed. He let himself ease up on his legs and was pretty sure, now that it was one in the morning, Billy Dawson hadn't come by on account of the Secret Service, the Navy Cadets, or any wing-beaked Lucero.

"So you're through, huh?" Lester asked, looking very interested. "I mean, the draft . . . they're . . ."

"What the hell're you bugging me for? . . . I said I'd tell you. . . . Yeah, I'm through. I did it. I'm out. And what's it to you?" Billy hated faggots worse than phlegm, with their veins up through their transparent skin like tracks up corduroy. He could smell them a mile off. Hell, Billy Dawson was cock of the campus and could have any cunt he wanted. Ask anybody.

I didn't say he couldn't, Lester said to himself, but then why's he here? At the foot of my bed with one knee propped up under his chin, and his clean white sweat socks and his pennies in his loafers?

"Guess I'll be shoving off," he said, but did he go?

Hell no, he didn't go anywhere, so Lester just let those legs of his slide underneath further until they felt the heart of Billy Dawson's perfect little flat ass, and if he could have any cunt on campus that still didn't mean he wanted any.

Toes like baby turtles, up/down, down/up. Lester Newbauer's fag toes, while Billy Dawson whispered, "Fuck off." Fuck off, three times because he was going out as clean as he'd come. As clean as a whistle, god-damn you. . . . As a hound's tooth, that's how clean, while Lester's wordless toe-fingers kept on under him as smooth as a shoehorn.

And then Billy leapt up. "You cocksucking, blood-sucking one-each whore," he screamed. "You filthy

· 63 ·

fucking faggot, go to hell on the black market." He gave Lester a lunging shove that sent him into shock as Billy tore on out of there, smoothing his hair back and slamming the door. Who the hell do you think you're sucking around with your toes like turtles?

Just who the hell do you think you're after? Sure as shit not Billy Dawson. Billy Dawson wiped his ass with razorblades. Billy Dawson had fought himself a couple of cows down Juarez way, carried more balls across the goal than Glenn Davis, wore golden gloves, was taller, blonder and more built than Ty Power in *Captain from Castille*. Ole BD, who two weeks before jumped off a freight train after, you bet your balls, conned not only the army but the big brass all the way up the navy's chain of command too. . . . Hell yes, that was Billy Dawson. What the hell did he take him for?

Tough? Billy Dawson ate ground glass sandwiches. The only one in the whole damn regiment, including the captain, who didn't brown his BVDs when the big navy transport suddenly split apart right over the parade field killing seven cadets just like that, filling the sky with iridescent pus. The only one who didn't figure it could have been him, the fear all over their foreheads thick as acne. . . . Big deal, Cadet Bill Dawson figured. . . . Another crash another Late Show: Gable and Tracy in *Test Pilot*. Billy Dawson would never see anybody else's number touching his. So Lester Newbauer could go stick his turtle toes up one of their asses, his was clean. And ready for anything. . . . So what, he said to the seven shitless wonders who the goddamned very next day ran like crazy to sign out of the program. . . . Because seven cadets went up and only seven crash helmets came down? Because somebody else got theirs? Jeeeesus, Billy Dawson told them. . . . Death always plays possum, it's all just a question of tipping your hat when he passed by, doing a fast little toe-step. What good will it do to hide among the swabbies? Had Destiny taken to riding a bicycle built for seven? But then Billy was used to success. It was his key to success. He always rose to the top.

He turned down Bernalillo, jamming his hands down his pockets and whistled "Papa Won't You Dance With Me." Down at Epsilon Epsilon somebody lobbed a hot bag of piss out a second story window. The university's beloved bronze founder in front of the Home Ec building was wearing a Modess Because belt and Billy had himself helped to tar and feather President Priestly's Chevy and then to hoist it up the side of Dillman Hall wrapped in toilet paper. Life was fun. He'd already conned Buick into fixing the fender on somebody else's cuff and screw the faggot.

He crossed the parking lot behind the Pharmacy Building and a dull distant ringing opened into a roar. There must have been a thousand sophomores in shetland sweaters and white bucks charging the side doors of Hokona, the girls' dorm. The girls themselves were hanging out the windows dropping brassieres and waving white flags with leg holes. Billy walked a little faster. Somebody played "Theeeaaahh Wheeeeaaaaaalll ooooof Fooooooortuuuune" on a portable and shouted, hubba hubba! Billy pulled back. His knees were shaking and he could still feel the silhouette of

Lester Newbauer's toes up his ass. Go on, he said, that's where the action is, get your keister on up there, and he did go, but not as fast as the rest of them.

"This one's for 'the gip,' " a guy with a chino hard-on hollered, and smashed a balloon filled with colored water against the old chandelier in the downstairs sitting room.

Mrs. Horn, the housemother, swore the barbarians had broken down the barricades, but Billy could see even from where he stood up against a poplar that her charges were begging for it, none more so than Amy Collins, upstairs in her room where she busily pressed a pair of cotton undies between the pages of her diary. Amy was a virgin. No, it was stronger than that. Amy Collins was virginal, and it stuck out all over her. So much so that it scared all comers away. Her voice. The way she held her swan's neck. The satin shine in her eyes. Amy Collins was *everyboy's* ideal. You didn't mess with the Amy Collinses in this world. They were even too good to be your sister.

Billy rolled himself a Bull Durham and took four good pulls. Mrs. Horn dragged her dresser in front of her bedroom door. In the distance you could hear a siren. Amy zipped her sweater a little lower about her breasts. She was breathing very heavily and couldn't wait for the action. Up and down the halls around her were the sounds of running feet, some painted on the toes like lollipops, a lot more in white bucks or cowboy boots. Billy could smell the virgins and the cunts in their crinolines, wet hair, and flannel nightgowns, throwing the stuff out the windows: the panties with the nylon roses and the slips with thread-tied baby's breath, while old Mrs. Housemother Horn huddled under her bed and stroked her empty titties that felt, even to her, like old linen change purses.

"Not you, dog biscuit," some engineer called to some art student, and Billy stood there sucking on his cigarette and leaning against the tree. He knew them all, those fat asses in there, what did he need it for? He watched the Kappa Thetas park a yellow convertible catty-corner on University Avenue so the cops would make a swell target for old condoms and rancid butter. He thought about Lester Newbauer, about moving on, and somebody threw down a 34-C in satin which got caught on his shoulder.

"Goldfish-eater," he murmured. He stepped on the cigarette and walked around to the front door. The screaming and tearing around rattled the whole building. He could hear doors slamming, rustling, and giggling. He spit into the fireplace and then went to the piano and picked out "Row, Row, Row Your Boat" with one finger.

The girls screamed "No," and the boys weren't taking no for an answer. "Gently down the stream," he played, and thought maybe a beer at The Pig's Eye was what was needed; but instead he pushed through the inner doors and watched Big Porgis throw a fat pink hand almost up a robe and then pull back as the girl just turned around and kept on leaving.

He saw Toolie Grey disappear into a mahogany doorway and heard the sound of the door lock. He felt himself pull away from the Tri Chis tearing through like so

many bowling pins, ass over ass. He was Mr. First
Nighter, by the wall telephone, up the stairs, down the
halls, with all the thwumping of corduroy right by him
like a radio play. Wooly arms, poplin jackets, all loaded
with tit harnesses and bush warmers. They waved
their booty over his head and shouted their battle cries
though his ears, and sometimes they nicked him on
their way and sometimes they gave him the good word.

Why did I come back? Billy asked himself. Maybe
I'm not cut out to be a college boy, as they screamed
on their way either up or down, everybody else so sure
their path led to buried treasure. He got to the landing and turned either right or left, what difference did
it make, doors ajar, drawers spilled on beds. Stockings
thrown aside like ugly women. Teddybears caught in
Tampax snowdrifts. Somebody said, "Hi, Dawson."
Somebody he once felt up behind the bleachers took
the occasion to grab his balls, and more bodies, all over
him, all around him, like a taffypull and a headache.

Up ahead a door was open. The room looked empty
but there was a stillness inside that he recognized. It
surrounded the slow movements of a girl and boy. So
slow it was as if they were caught in a tableau on glass.
The girl was standing up on the bed with one arm
behind her, holding her brassiere shut, and the guy had
both arms out, like he was balancing himself on a pipe
fence. He had a tight backbone and was ready to
spring, as he'd once watched his father's cat, ready to
spring on the cornered mouse. He was watching the
girl's every breath, blocking her every way, and it was,
to Billy, interesting. He wasn't sure exactly what was

going on. How much she was enjoying it. How serious it all was, or why, either way, he gave a flying fuck.

She tried to move further back against the wall but was already flush. The guy in the orange ski sweater held a broom handle. No broom. Just the stick part, and his face was red. Every time she took a step to the side, so did he.

Without seeing the guy's face, Billy could tell *he* was serious anyway. He was edging closer and closer until he nudged the iron frame of her bed. A quick feint to his left which made her jump. And the girl watching his every move with the biggest turquoise eyes in the world. They never blinked. They just stared at him. Two dips of pistachio surrounded by black mink, waiting for her tormentor to pounce, and never even noticing Billy. That part intrigued him. There she stood in a skirt and a bra, like a Vargas girl against the window shade, and never even smelled him.

Her breathing was heavy and the guy with the stick said, "I'm not going to hurt you." He moved closer again as he said it. And it was then that Billy was sure she was in it as deep as the guy with the broom handle. They were playing a game with each other, a game where everybody won.

Amy sucked up her breath and posed herself carefully. Now Billy wasn't so sure she hadn't seen him. She blew stray bits of hair out of her eyes. He leaned against the doorway and watched as the guy got an arm up her skirt. "Oh God," he heard her moan, "this is it, I swear it." And then he was on her, pressing himself on her body, evenly, leaving nothing unattended to. She fell down as if to sink her teeth into his shoulder but no blood came. She wrestled, but spread herself out at the same time, whipping her head back and forth so that it made her hair frothy and her eyes large. She steadied the bottoms of her feet against the bedstead and was very, very quiet.

The guy pulled at her shoulder straps and unzipped when Billy decided enough was enough. The whole thing was too pat, going too easily according to plan. It irritated him. One minute he was still the spectator and the next he'd thrown himself on the guy's ski sweater, pulled him off the bed, and was beating the shit out of him. Out of the side of his eye he thought he was aware of the girl giving a quick anguished cry. Of the motion of her legs, pulling together with frustration. But he wasn't sure he'd even noticed her at all. He heard the thud of the guy's body and saw him pull a little to the side as if to protect his privates. He socked him a good one in the mouth in case he thought about begging for him to go easy. His head bobbled around on his trunk as if it were out of joint. His arms were flinging around uselessly, and Billy socked him again. The more he hit him, the madder he got, but at whom he wasn't sure. Outside the running feet and the shouting got louder and louder, and he realized the guy under him was looking up at him with a kind of recognition. He'd even rolled a little to one side so that Billy hit into the floor.

"Take it easy," he said. "What can they do to you?" And when Billy stopped socking and cocked his head, Jack took his moment and ran with it. He picked up his stick and used it as a cane, down the hallway and the staircase. Billy didn't even see him go. He was listening to the voice of President Priestly over the campus police amplifier.

"Ladies and gentlemen," the president of the university said. "Ladies and gentlemen, we are giving you ten minutes." Billy looked down again and wondered what he'd meant, what could who do to him? The girl was looking at him. He could feel her turquoise eyes through his blazer.

"It will be necessary to use tear gas to evacuate the building if you do not cooperate," he heard. He turned around and saw her on the bed, and behind her, through the window, the cop car with Priestly himself on top with a megaphone in his hand. A running crowd of kids waving girls' underwear streamed out the dorm doors and ran through the lawn where the car was parked. Another car came across the parking lot at sixty to herd them along like television dogies.

The girl lay there trembling. She'd shaken out her hair so that it fell just right . . . a little bit between her breasts, a little over her pillow. This one, all Snow White, all cream to the touch, was nothing like the twat from the taco joint the other night, one hip high in the air, hollowed, and rounded and ready as anything. She moved her bottom around and around in a small circle.

"You have five minutes," they heard through the megaphone.

"Please," Amy whispered. She rose off the bed and sank back. Her arms were out and her breasts fell apart and vibrated before settling back into place again. Billy watched her and waited to see what he was going to do.

"Please," she said again.

The running, stamping, stomping noises in the halls throbbed through his brain. The distant call of the PA system, the girl's desperate pleading, her arms growing longer and whiter every moment. "Please . . . ," and he opened his mouth to say something. He turned the palms of his hands up to the ceiling.

"I'm sorry." He heard himself say it. He reached over and touched the smooth of her hip, then he quickly picked up a pair of her cotton underpants and jammed them into his pocket, opened her window and lightly jumped the distance down to the parking lot below. God help me, he moaned. Keep me from the bedroom that smells like last week.

"Don't go," Amy Collins called after him. She knelt at the window ledge and watched him sprint across the lawn and past the campus police car. "Why do you have to go?" she cried. Then she fell back on her mattress and tried to pry out her stainless steel hymen with a can opener. She'd been so sure college life was going to be her answer. That once she entered the portals of Hokona Hall she'd fall rapidly, but perhaps that was because Amy Collins didn't take into consideration that in Navajo, Hokona means "The Hall of the Virgin Butterflies."

· 11 ·

THIS TIME WHEN LESTER'S
front door pushed open he knew who it was, and instead of scaring himself with fantasies of the FBI, held
the covers up so Billy Dawson could bury himself in
them.

"It's not like the measles," Lester promised him,
"now, now. No dots, no telltale signs of anything, don't
worry, everything will be all right," but he could see the
anguish in Billy's eyes as he let himself, at first, be
taken, and then, as they went along, took what he
wanted for himself. "I won't tell anybody; you knew you
could count on me," Lester crooned and finally Billy
kicked off his loafers, pulled back the covers, and tore
off the sash to Lester's limp, smelly terry.

It was the worst moment in Billy's life and he knew it and he loved it, both at the same time. Why, he screamed to himself, couldn't it have been the girl with the pistachio eyes, who was as clean as the whistle he would have preferred to have been himself. Fucky, fucky, suck, suck, he fell on Lester and Lester on him, all over the sheets and the clothes and themselves, and up it popped, he saw it, down there, his it, like a new-born stringbean through the wet grass. At attention, at last. For the first time ever, there he was doing it, 2, 4, 6, 8 / Who do we appreciate?

He'd torn out of Hokona and sprinted back across Hermosilla, past Lead, down Sycamore, and finally over to Elm, only because he had to. He'd fallen on the freckled receptacle and broken his geyser on him, he'd pulled on everything that moved, like so many kid's birthday firecrackers, fringed at both ends. . . . He'd kept his eyes closed and his mind stoppered, yet here he was on top of the whore cunt faggot, damn his eyes, sucking his blood like a mewling infant, he hated himself. Yet there he was, no shit, for the first time breaking his water pipe all the hell over everything. His swollen, throbbing water pipe, pouring, spewing, and streaming out all over Lester, his sheets, his blankets, him, them . . . all over everything with more and more frantic pulsing starts. Like a motor caught on a hill forever between gears. Billy could hear himself screaming. He could see their fingers pointing at him. He could hear Leadbelly roll me over, jam it in, and do it again. It was screaming and horrible and it made him puke and he wanted it again. He'd waited and put it off and turned his back on it and couldn't live with it and he wanted it and wanted it and wanted more.

"You bastard," he retched into Lester's ear. He sobbed and came one tiny bit more into the soft body that gave up only freckles. "You sonofabitchin' bastard," as his chest was wracked with a sobbing, heavenly terror all mixed up into one sour stew.

"Come on, Billy," Lester moaned and tried patting his hair. "It's all right, I promise . . . I'll never tell," he promised. "Nobody will ever know," and Billy pulled back like an adder and then reached into his back pocket and pulled out the bright shine of a penknife. Lester sucked his breath in and pulled away.

"Don't be an ass, Dawson. For crissakes." But it wasn't Lester Billy was after. Before Lester could, one last time, assure Billy of his honorable intentions, Billy had slashed a perfect little cross over his own left tit, in as far as it would go. Lester hunched up his shoulders and shook his head as the rivulets of hot blood spurted down the beautiful chest onto the still throbbing bone between his legs where it stippled pink on the tops of the white hairs.

Billy made no move to wipe away the blood. He didn't even look down as the gouged-out flesh hung there bottoms up, raw and bubbled, dripping penance. He only turned away from Lester and shuddered again.

"You filthy fucking faggot," he said, staring at his own traitorous knees.

"Look, Dawson," Lester said, "I mean it, one lousy

time? Everybody's had his quick roll in a stranger's rack. I swear to God," he said, which was when they heard the knock at the front door.

Lester sat up sharply and was surprised. Ron wouldn't knock. Billy dashed into the bathroom carrying his pants and Trini Lucero called out, "You? Lester Newbauer? You wrote my name on your poster! How could you? What makes you think I want to be saved?"

· 12 ·

THE REST OF TRINI LUCERO'S
brothers and sisters were born Mexican-Americans.
Trini was born guilty. Somehow nothing he ever did,
even and including his pinnacle achieved in the Alameda High School's Forensic Society, ever brought the
bloom to the brown cheeks of his father, Ysofio Lucero-
Casadas, M.D.

Trini was fat, had round shoulders and a mouth so
full of extra teeth it was hard for him to close it; but his
father wasn't so hot on his siblings, either, the sisters
who spent so much of the time crossing themselves, or
the boys, who, the doctor always said, couldn't any of
them look at him with both eyes at the same time. Still,
the brothers and sisters revered their father and hon-

ored their sainted mother's memory without need of the Alameda High School's Forensic Society. Trini had joined because the doctor thought it might, though he doubted it, give the little *cabron* some *cajones*.

Trini's father didn't even live with them in the big brown house in El Paso. He stayed with his big chi-chied mistress in Juarez and left strict instructions for his Mexican-American offspring to make the track team, keep chintz curtains on the kitchen windows, and never go across the border for anything . . . not oranges, gas, or even leather belts. The children lived with Lugardita Moya, who was once described by a family friend as a Catholic's Catholic.

In Trini's whole round-shouldered life, except for the one time it had been his turn to sentence somebody else to the hemlock, he'd never even known what it was to get the extra piece of pie. All Trini had ever really known was what it felt like to have one fat thigh rub against another. Nobody could convince Trini that guilt wasn't part of the package. Guilt was the glue in the peanut butter, the cartilege that held his soul to-gether. Yes, Socrates had gotten what was coming to him, but so had he, and he didn't mind who knew it.

"Don't ever let me hear you talk like that again," Mort was heard to say to Trini, lifting him up by his lapels and pressing wet Clara Bow lips to his pimpled cheek. "You are not alone in this world. You have us." He also said, "We will see you through," but not until he read Lester's poster in the library, wrote down his address and swore if he did nothing else he would personally save this persecuted Mexican, or die trying.

· 13 ·

Lester Newbauer's screen door to the darkened living
room. His forehead looked like a waffle iron, pressed
so long against the screen, and he still couldn't see
anything.

"Couldn't you have even had the decency to find out
first? Ask a person if they want to be saved?"

There were tears of rage on his cheeks but he'd made
up his mind to start clearing his name and clear it he
would. At least with the Board of Education. Make sure
they knew he approved of their action, applauded their
vigilance. These were perilous times. He didn't want
them thinking he couldn't see that these were perilous
times.

"Mr. Lucero?" Lester called from the kitchen sink, into which he was busy peeing because Billy was locked in his bathroom.

"Just a minute, Mr. Lucero . . . I'm coming. . . ."

"Didn't it even occur to you how it would look to the Board?" Trini called. "How do you think it looks? How?" Trini called again.

"Just a minute," Lester begged him, over the sound of the faucet. "I can explain everything, if you can just wait a minute."

"There," he sighed to himself. He closed his robe, hesitated a minute at the bathroom door, which was still and obviously locked, and didn't know what else to do besides face the consequences of his rash action, in the flesh.

Trini let himself slide down the front of the screen. His buttons made a noise like a xylophone against the grid of the mesh.

"Oh my God," Lester moaned.

Trini said, down around his legs somewhere, "I don't, I don't want to be saved. Can't you understand that?"

Lester knelt next to him. "You don't what?"

"Saved," he said. "I don't want to be saved. I never wanted to be saved. What's the matter with you? Why did you think I wanted to? I told them. Don't you listen to the radio? They asked me and I said that the Board of Education knows best. Doesn't that mean anything? A man's word. I gave them my word. . . ."

He said "Board of Education" like an old art professor of Lester's used to say "Masaccio." And then Trini began a kind of rhythmic banging of his head against the bottom of the screen. "Oh God," Lester said again, cursing himself for his misplaced idealism. "I can't tell you. No, I really can't . . . You know how sorry I am and everything. . . . How . . ." His voice dropped as he found himself looking over Trini's blue serge shoulder into the street, where a very large fellow got out of a wooden station wagon held together with carpet tacks. The fellow was singing, "Eighteen bottles of beer on the wall, eighteen bottles of beer," and was looking through the pockets of the George Raft suit jacket he was wearing. Ashley had told Mort she couldn't come with him because she had a headache, when actually it was because of Genero Mendola. Genero was only a kid, maybe seventeen, and as ribby as a desert hyena, but when all of a sudden, two weeks ago last Thursday, there he was, what was she supposed to say? No?

"They'll think I was in on it, can't you see that? They'll think I can't be trusted," Trini blubbered, banging his head slower and slower because it was beginning to hurt.

"No, you're right," Lester said without really paying attention, as the big man finally dug out a child's copybook from the baggy bulges of the pants that had never matched the jacket even in their first life.

"But what'll I do if they think I was in on it? You know . . ."

"For heaven's sake," Lester said, finally looking down at him. "You're already fired, man, what else can they do to you?"

"Fired . . . that's all you people know. What about honor? About my word? Doesn't my word count for anything?" While outside the big fellow had opened the copybook with slow and elaborate movements and was running an enormous index finger across every line and down every page. He had somehow hypnotized Lester, who could no longer take his eyes off him, watching the way he didn't exactly move his mouth with the motions of his finger, but almost. Lester continued to watch as Trini, too, lifted his head just in time for Mort to look up with a jack-o'-lantern expression on his rosy face. Then Lester heard himself moan, "What the hell have I done?" When it was all obviously too late to stop the grinning man as he turned to wave at them, to shake a little black and white notebook up and down in the air, and to point ridiculously to what would be Lester's address copied down from one of the several posters he had in his madness tacked up those many moons before. He could feel the big man thunder toward them as the ground shook, as he threw open his arms toward the cringing Trini still lying there all over the porch.

The two of them, Lester and Trini, each with his own premonitions, watched Mort shake his hairy head back and forth, cluck his tongue, and throw open his checkerboard arms.

"So that was the fellow they were trying to make into a lampshade," Mort clucked, pointing at Trini. The two others felt his eyes water all the way from the fading safety of the porch and in one moment both Lester and Trini, each in his own separate way, wished he were dead.

Mort approached seven leagues at a step, with compassion and succor enough for a multitude of Trinidad Luceros. Before Trini could even think of fending him off, he could feel himself being lifted from his knees and pressed mercilessly into a Goodwill Industries bosom. Mort then held him at arm's length and drew him close again. Trini could hear the small bones in his upper vertebrae crack one after another.

Then Lester felt himself kissed on both cheeks, and the two of them were carried forcibly out of the hot sun and into Lester's living room. The saving of Trinidad Lucero had begun. Lester Newbauer only hoped Ron Harkness didn't decide to come home for a tunafish sandwich.

"I can't tell you fellahs how glad I am to know you," Mort said. He told them his full name. He said his wife would have been there had it been humanly possible and then he slapped them both so affectionately on their backs that Lester worried for his lungs and Trini swore if he got out with his sin, he'd make an immediate Novena to St. Job.

Mort, of course, naturally assumed that they were idealists in the old Eugene V. Debs tradition and his eyes filled again as he held Trini at arm's distance and told him earnestly that every American had a right to a free and open tribunal.

"And I'm here to see that you get one," he told him. This was when he raised Trini by his lapels, kissed his cheek, and told him he was not alone.

After he again swore his eternal allegiance to the cause of Trini's freedom from persecution, Trini's heart turned to pulque. He, of all people, knew what *they* and their *ilk* meant by free and open tribunals. He didn't need *their* help.

But while Lester worried about Ron Harkness coming home and while Trini just tried to stay out of the reach of the herringbone Hercules, on the other side of the bathroom keyhole, the sound of Mort Dralon's voice rang another bell. *The* bell. The bell that sounded the beginning of what Billy Dawson had come to think of as ROUND TWO.

He squinted through the keyhole to get a more perfect view, to make absolutely sure . . . but all he'd so far been able to make out clearly was a tight little blue dot that turned out to be Trini Lucero's asshole.

"I told you before, you have a negative attitude," Mort said when Trini pulled his arm out of an embrace, and said, "Guilt is a matter of personal preference."

Then Trini said, "How do you know? Were you there? How do you know I don't get my orders all the way from Moscow, Russia?"

To this Mort said only, "Pshaw!"

Trini looked helplessly at Lester, who was buttering a piece of rye bread with caraway seeds, even though he knew he'd be sorry later on. He always kept one eye out the window. The other one on the door to the bathroom.

"Look," he finally said to Mort, "Mr. Lucero is right. After all, we have no right to save a man against his will. It's just not the American way."

Trini smiled at him and Lester turned away quickly so he didn't have to acknowledge it. He could not anymore, even if he tried, remember how he'd come to be so involved in the first place. Why, just because he needed a poster for class, he'd lettered, SAVE LUCERO, instead of, for instance, ONLY YOU CAN PREVENT FOREST FIRES.

"No, we are brothers," Mort was saying earnestly. "Together we can move mountains, together, you and I," which was when Trini banged both fists against his chest.

"Don't you see that I did it. I did it," he screamed, "and I meant to do it. I'd even do it again. I am guilty," he said. "Are you deaf or something? I've been tried, sentenced, and convicted. I deserved it. Because of, listen to me, damn you. . . . You're not . . ." He banged again on Mort's chest, as the big man smiled down benevolently. "Because of me America sleeps a little sounder. I'm not afraid. And . . . And," he screamed, "and nobody is going to take that medicine away from me. Can you understand that? Nobody!!!"

"Oh God," Lester moaned, stuffing caraway seeds down a very small throat. "I never dreamed . . . I never . . ."

"Trinidad," Mort began. "You don't mind if I call you Trinidad? Here, Trinidad," he said, "sit down," and he leaned against the trembling blue figure till it seemed to melt into the chair. "You see, Trinidad, the question of right and wrong is bigger than both of us. We here in this room can't begin to grasp the magnitude . . . the enormity of . . . Trinidad, do you realize that without your cooperation, what hope is there for the struggling millions? Think of India, Trinidad, do you realize . . . and what about China? Do you think they have it easy over there, Trinidad? Don't you see?"

Oh, Trini saw all right. That Commy symp wasn't fooling anyone. He could say "millions" all he wanted, but the word was "masses." Trini Lucero wasn't born yesterday, you know. He knew about Karl Marx. And he knew he had to get out of there. China? One more word about China and he'd send an anonymous letter to Henry Cabot Lodge. . . .

Lester could only agree with him, even if he was a liberal. When it came to China . . . and even if Ron were only half right. If the telephone didn't have a tap on it. The walls still had ears, you know, and always had.

"What are you, some kind of Communist?" Lester said, just in case. No harm in setting his own record as straight as he could at this late date. But Mort's face was shining with the radiance of a true believer and part-time defender of unrequited faiths. "Don't you see, Trinidad? Thou hast been tried, sentenced, and punished without benefit of jury, of a hearing by your peers. Us, Trinidad," he said, pointing dramatically around the room and almost knocking over Ron's favorite Tlingit foot fetish. "We are your peers. Your brothers. Trust me," he said imploringly, but Trini only shook his head.

"Guilty," he murmured every once in a while. "Leave me alone. I'm as guilty as they come."

"Not guilty, Trinidad. You're confused, you're . . ."

"Don't tell me," the smaller man suddenly screamed. "I tell you I can prove it. I know my rights. Don't try

· 86 ·

and tell me my rights, damn it. That's a laugh. Oh, that's a good one. Yessir, I know my damn rights as well as anybody and . . ."

"You see?" Mort said shaking his big head, inclining it toward Lester, who was washing down the caraway seeds with Sebella, and still Billy Dawson in the bathroom wasn't sure. "Move over," he whispered into the wrong side of the door. But he didn't, the body that went with the familiar voice. It just stood there, just that much out of eyeshot.

"It's a question of American jurispru . . ."

"Screw American jurispru, the bastard tells you he's guilty. The sonofabitch ought to know if he's guilty I suppose. For crissakes move over so we can get on with it," but Mort had his pinkies jammed down his ears, just in case it was wax that had turned his world into a Japanese movie with Sanskrit subtitles. Why? he said to himself. Why wouldn't he just lie down and let Mort do what was good for him? Trini needed him. Didn't he see he needed him?

United we stand! and
Shoulders to the wheel!

Lester rolled a fingerful of peanut butter into a raw tortilla and washed them down with aspirin.

And don't forget the wheel of oppression. Or the men of good will holding hands into adversity? Didn't they know anything?

Did they think a champion of the underdog could so easily be brushed aside? Is that what they thought?

· 87 ·

No! Mort Dralon had made up his mind. Trinidad Lucero, victim, would be saved all right. It was the only way. He reached for him, pulling gently, over the footstool, past the Somerset Maugham chair, and on the Indian rug with the aniline dye.

"Can't you see, Trinidad? *A person has certain unalienable rights whether he likes it or not!!*"

"Not *unalienable*," Lester said into his eggnog. "A person has certain *in*alienable rights."

"See?" Mort said, triumphant, "he knows!! See, Trinidad. . . . A person can't just go around ignoring his unalienable rights, right and left. A person . . ." but when he said "person," he moved a little to the left, which put him right smack into the bull's-eye of Billy Dawson's keyhole. Less than a second later the door swung open and out sprang Billy. *El Guero*, defender of his own inalienable rights. This time, right of access, punching away before the door had even been kicked aside. Socking and punching at the stunned head flung back and forth on its neck like the severed Gorgon's.

"The greaser's right," he said, getting a cross jab into the eye he'd been waiting for. It was a goddamn free country all right, and the goddamn greaser had a goddamn right to take whatever goddamn medicine the . . .

The hairy stalwart's head just sort of smiled distantly. Once, after it had hit the floor, it rose and said, "The pride of unborn generations," and then whipped over to the other side as Billy socked it again. And Billy didn't stop socking until the entire body began writhing around on the floor like a broken leg.

Trini watched the entire proceedings with some confusion and a mingling of several other emotions. Now that nobody was stopping him, he made no move to leave. He stayed a long time. Till long after Billy dusted himself off, adjusted his jacket, combed his hair, and got ready to leave. And he was glad he had, because, before leaving, and after wiping his hands and smiling the blond avenger said if Trini's unconscious tormentor ever bugged his ass again, he could call on him. He even wrote down his name and address, which Trini took, still trembling, folded in four places, and saved carefully in his wallet.

The day after the panty raid, Amy Collins spent the best part of the morning mourning the loss of her two almost-rapists. Then she tried calling her daddy on the telephone. But her daddy wasn't home. She went home but her daddy wasn't there. Her daddy was standing in front of his best friend's crapper with his cock in his hands, too scared to either pee or let go. Her daddy was the Legislative Guild Representative of Trinidad Lucero's ex-school, and Trinidad Lucero had been trying to get him on the phone all day too. It was all more than the L. G. R. could bear.

Dave Collins, Trini Lucero's ex-Legislative Guild Representative, had a sinking feeling. He had it even before the phone started ringing, and as it turned out, going to his best friend's to get away from it all hadn't helped.

Dave Collins was afraid. He was afraid of his relationship with Trini Lucero in the halls on the way to the teacher's lounge, How ya been? How's life treating you, and all of that—but the real fear in Dave Collins's life went back a lot further than Trini Lucero.

He'd already been in his friend's john twenty minutes. There on his friend's toilet lid, his friend had pasted a colored glossy of Joseph McCarthy waving a maddened fist. The fist seemed to Dave to be aimed at him personally. Behind the Senator's head, on the toilet bowl, two candles flickered menacingly and under McCarthy's messianic visage his friend had printed the words: OUR FATHER OF THE SHIT HOUSE. And besides, his friend was sleeping with Dave's wife, Dell. Dave Collins was dry.

Dave's eyes had kept him out of World War II, but by the time the "Korean conflict" rolled around, he was hardly even wearing reading glasses. Because his eyes got better, he got drafted. The army took him and then called him their old man, assigned him to a bunch of keys that didn't seem to open anything, and he spent two years like tits on a boar. His wife Dell called their existence implausible, and said only a loser would end up at his age with ten pounds of keys around his waist. So Dell assed around a lot and the army spent its time investigating Dave. Maybe, he'd often speculated, if they hadn't assigned him to Tiheras Valley, New Mexico, his life might have been different. Fort Leonard Wood, Missouri, maybe, where they'd have fitted him for a rifle, sent him over to Korea and blown his brains out. . . . Anything. But at Tiheras, the army looked into his high school days as David Cooperstein. As Mama's pride and joy. And the family business that

Dave eventually ran away from. They even found out that Pa had kept Dave's going to college away from Ma. They found out that Dave's Ma had wanted him to stay in diamonds. "What's so terrible about diamonds?" she used to say, but all the time Dave wanted to go into guidance, so that finally Pa used to tell Ma the boy was cutting prisms like an angel when all the time he was graduating from CCNY, changing his name, and getting cheated on an engagement ring for Dell Horowitz which turned out to be a rhinestone.

At first, when Dave realized he was being followed, he figured it was because of his name. What else could it be? He never signed a petition in his life, and when it came to the Haymarket Affair, he couldn't tell an anarchist from an emerald cut. But whatever, whenever he looked around, there he was, this guy in a belted raincoat, trailing him all the time no matter what. No matter where he was going, for better than four months, rain or shine. . . . If he bought a Coke or took a leak, all he had to do was look around and there he'd be. A guy about twenty, with a crew cut, who carried a notebook and a tiny cigarette lighter that turned out to be a camera. One day, a buddy of his, a guy named Jaffee, from Englewood, really scared him. He'd called him over and told him from behind the palm of his hand that he'd seen movies of him coming out of the base library, carrying a book.

A book? Oh God, what book? *Nightwood? Manhattan Transfer?* What had he taken out that fateful evening? And why movies all of a sudden?

He lay awake three nights running and discovered

that his beautiful wife Dell, when she slept home at all, which wasn't often, snored. But Dell, right then, wasn't the issue. The issue was what. What he had done, what? While his wife was out humping everything in khaki? And still the young fellow with a notebook was behind him. He even found out his name was Ronald Croonquist. It got so Dave took to waiting for him mornings in case he'd overslept. Eventually Dave Collins started talking to himself. At night his wife imagined that somebody else was there in bed with them and for a while that sparked an interest in her husband she hadn't had in years, but Dave still suffered.

Actually, the surveillance had very little to do with David Cooperstein Collins. The Army tailed Collins because of the cell that met in the fiction stacks in the library and passed secret notes under the due dates in the little envelopes, who did they think they were kidding? Sigrid Undset, the army's ass. And not only Dave Collins. There were four other readers on the base too, so that besides Ronald Croonquist, the army employed three other busy little shadows. One of the men they followed was Ted Andresson and on his birthday his mother sent him a Picasso to hang up over his footlocker and his cousin sent him a card: ROSES ARE RED AND SO ARE YOU, ha . . . ha . . . ha . . ., which didn't do Andressen any good either.

After a while the army decided there was no secret, message-passing Communist cell in the fiction stacks in the library and so they quit following Dave Collins, Ted Andresson, and the two other guys, but Corporal Collins, né Cooperstein, never adjusted. Dave Collins had come to depend on Ronald Croonquist. He had become a fixed constant in his rootless world. He looked forward to Ronald Croonquist watching him eat his poached eggs on whole wheat, and when he woke one morning to find himself once more another of the unmarked nonentities in this world, he broke.

After the "conflict," Dell read a book about psychology and found out that Dave was suffering from acute paranoia. She also found out that change triggered it off, for instance when Dave was discharged from the army altogether and had to start wearing civvies again. Or this business of getting out of bed in the morning whenever he damn well pleased. The transition was too much of a shock, so he just stayed put, called the bedpan his loving cup, and imagined he and Ronald Croonquist were playing chess under the covers. But that was all a thing of their past. Now Dave was a respectable schoolteacher—even a school official.

Dave opened the door of the john, peeked out and Dell was gone. So was his best friend. Well, everybody had his cross, and at least, when it came to her habits, there were no surprises. It was the other things that got to Dave Collins, the abrupt disruptions in his everyday routine. For instance, right now, this Trini Lucero trouble.

Dell had talked him into taking the job as Legislative Guild Representative of Tiheras Valley Junior High School, where, up until recently, Lucero taught band instruments. It was all Dell's fault, he worried, sitting there smiling. As Legislative Guild Representative he'd have to attend the hearing. He'd have to be there, know charge by charge what Trinidad Lucero's transgressions amounted to, and it scared the hell out of him. When it came to contagious diseases, Communistic leanings were the worst . . . And now the *Herald* calling Trinidad Lucero a traitor? Something might rub off when he went to the hearing. He knew about lists and how even if it looked like your name was erased, all they had to do was squeeze a little lemon juice on the old spot and they had you again. Even being in the same room at the hearing was dangerous. Legislative Guild Representative or not . . . official capacity or not. . . . He gave final obeisance to Senator McCarthy's shrine, wished his wife would finish screwing so they could go home, and zipped up.

New Mexcio, 1953, the hiding place of the atom bomb. Buried under the many long purpled rock ranges through the deserts and towns, the bombs were out of sight but not mind. Wherever you went, on a bus, to the Court Cafe, for a gibson at the Alvarado . . . the bomb went with you, and to make sure you didn't say a word about it, there were the Ronald Croonquists, behind clipboards and Alan Ladd raincoats. Civilian Ronald Croonquists, army Ronald Croonquists, and atomic energy Ronald Croonquists. Always over a shoulder and always on guard for that careless flippancy or passionate intimacy so they could put down your name and serial number on a list that would follow you forever.

It was a funny time to either teach or go to school. It was a funny time to just pick up a movie magazine or buy a bobby sock. Vintage pickings for Gilbert and Sullivan, 1953 New Mexico; an entire state walking around on tiptoes. But it didn't help. Nobody escaped the atomic fingerprint on the jugular anyhow.

Dell Collins sang *"Las Mañanitas"* out of tune on the way home in the Collins's VW. Dave said, "Nice party, wasn't it?" When they turned down Placitas, she was drumming her fingers on the dash and his foot was so heavy on the gas pedal she was afraid they'd crash right through the newly poured concrete on their look-alike adobe walk. Through the picture window their daughter Amy was seen sitting at the dining room table finishing up the leftover from dinner with her fingers.

"For heaven's sake, Amy," her mother said.

"Leave the child alone," her father said. "How come you're home?"

"I'm back. Who's Trini Lucero? He wants you to call him back," and she was down the hall without seeing her message hit her father like a depth charge. Yes, she was back. But she didn't want to talk about it. She might never even go out in the street again, she wasn't sure. She'd think it over.

"I knew it." He fell over a chair and then in it.

"Forgodsakes," Dell said. "I wonder what she means, 'she's back.'" She picked up the bowl and shuddered at her eldest child's fingerprints fossilized in the beans. She didn't want her to be back. She wanted her almost married and out of her hair. "You're letting this Lucero thing get out of hand." Sniveler, she murmured. One lousy phone call and they might as well have served a subpoena. She went into the kitchen.

Down the hall, **Amy** had her eyelids pressed to the mirror. She was staring at the fine red veins that meshed across the surfaces. She wondered how many good years she had left. She dropped her sweatshirt in a heap and cupped her breasts. Her good friend M.T. said that more than a handful was wasted, so she turned sideways to see how much, if any, was left over. If she didn't meet anybody in the next two weeks, she decided, the only course left would be suicide, but not before accosting anybody. Your penis or your life! She didn't care what, but a dead virgin she would never be. . . .

"Did it ever occur to you," Dell said, "he just might be. You know . . . well, I don't know. Maybe he is a Communist."

"Nobody understands me," Dave murmured.

Maybe I'll meet a real rapist, Amy thought. Three strikes against him, with saliva all over his chin.

"I waited almost an hour for you at the party," Dell walked out without answering him. When she came back for the cups she said, "I had a headache."

"Went to lie down maybe?"

"Maybe."

"I suppose Jay had a headache, too."

"I really have no idea what Jay had, too," she said. She took the salt and pepper into the kitchen.

"One of these days," Dave said, but when she came back, Dell just leaned against the table and looked at him with one of her withering looks.

"Why don't you save your threats for the seventh

grade, David. . . . My dance card seems to be all filled up."

From all the way in her room, Amy could feel her Daddy's eyes float up to the stucco ceiling, which meant his next line would be the one about his finally having had it. Then he'd say Jay Pickering was the last straw, and after a while he'd sigh plaintively and wonder when it was going to be his turn to have a little fun around there. Once her mother said, "What do I have to do, David, cut it off before I get a rise out of you?" but tonight they skipped the coda and went right on upstairs where he'd start right in on her boobs. Dell would sigh. Then she'd run her fingers through Dave's thinning hair and wonder aloud, beating her breast, how she went on the way she did.

Amy lay on her back and listened. Then she turned on her side and squeezed her nipples through her fingers. Her legs rubbed back and forth like a humming cricket and she told herself to hang on, it couldn't be long now. O.K., Hokona didn't work, something else would come along, there were a hell of a lot of fallen women lying around, look at Ida Lupino. . . .

She listened to her parents' bed squeak and then to the sounds of her father sitting up the rest of the night worrying. About being noticed at the Committee Hearing for Trinidad Lucero. About the repercussions of peeing on Joseph McCarthy. About her mother's annoying habit of humping anything that moved. Then she wondered when it would get around to being her turn, counted ten clitoral twitches, and fell asleep.

· 14 ·

ASHLEY DROVE INTO AL-
buquerque to collect her unconscious husband in her
lover's pickup. As she stared out the window she found
herself going over and over bits of long-ago advice from
her mother. "I've had all kinds, sweetie," she had said,
"and believe me, one swinging dick turns out to be
pretty much like another." Ashley looked quickly at
the sullen boy huddled around the steering wheel and
silently admitted to herself that the old bitch had called
it again. But Thalia Clukis had also told her something
inside was better than empty, which prompted another
worry. Was what she and this Genero Mendola had a
real affair? Did it count? She just couldn't figure out at

what point it stopped being just another piece of her ass.

They couldn't go any faster because the lights on the truck would go out the minute they went over thirty. Something to do with the generator, he said. She remembered because it was so rare he said anything. From the first he'd never been what you could call a talker. Even the first time, when she'd looked up from the lunch table where she'd been sitting doodling with the bits of left over rose hips and found him standing next to the icebox. At first she'd thought maybe the dark, scowling boy had come to deliver some goat's milk, but when she watched him unzip his fly and shake his thing at her, she became suspicious. Then, afterwards, when he was lying on top of her on the floor he still didn't say anything. Not even "thank you," or to tell her his name or anything, and it made her nervous. That was really the worst of it, not so much the quick wiggle inside, which she was used to, but the long, drawn-out absence of sound. That was the part which made her doubt the status of her affair.

At first she was nervous about his coming, but he seemed to know just when it was safe, so after a while she stopped worrying. At least it was something different from the constant Israel hassle she and Mort were always having.

Ashley would say "Rhile was only a baby. How could he remember the Negev?" It was ridiculous, hounding him. "Doesn't Frijolito look like the Negev?" Mort would say.

"Leave the boy alone," she'd say, but the boy's father was sure that the boy had sucked up the milk and honey of his homeland through his arteries. Not that he expected her to understand. Naturally.

"This is America," she kept finding herself saying, while he kept finding himself saying, "Yea though ye shall walk through the shadow of the valley of the Golan Heights."

"Sure, you remember," he'd say to the furry child. "That was in Israel, remember Israel, Rhile? Where you were born? Where you used to have so much fun growing tall and strong in the sun? Developing a healthy mind and a healthy body?" The child would nod frantically, throwing his big head back and forth, and the father would stand admiringly while Ashley ate another desiccated liver pill.

When they were first married, Ashley had nodded too. It had all seemed indisputable, the way her new husband could look through the arch at Washington Square and see all the way to the Mandelbaum Gate. A future jammed with horizons, he promised her, in the Promised Land, he promised. Then why, she wondered, did he knock her up their first night on the high seas? Even if it was important their offspring be born on Jewish soil, what was the hurry? He acted like it was a two-week junket, hotel included, pinning her to cabin class with his great knotted shillelagh jamming back and forth inside her, in a panic, not as he'd promised a full life, filled with challenge.

And since then it was the Inquisition.

"After all, Ashley, he was born there."

Did she say he wasn't?

"I was, Mommy, wasn't I? Wasn't that where I was born?"

"You resent it that the boy is Jewish, even though you don't say it, but you resent it anyway. It's understandable. Don't you? Don't you resent it?" That's all he ever talked about anymore, which was just about when Ashley started writing her brother Edgar.

Ashley mailed the first letter in October, which, if she thought about it, was before Mort's math class rolled the Pontiac down into the culvert and even before Genero Mendola.

"It's just that I wouldn't want him to forget it. The feel of the mornings. The smell of the fields. It's important to the boy, isn't it, Rhiley? Isn't it important?" And then he'd hold his hand and they'd look at each other, Mutt and Mutt.

"I was there too buddy," she said, "don't tell me about the land of your fathers. I worked the same sixteen-hour day as you did. I went to bed hungry and woke up worse. Why don't you tell the boy how the land of your fathers spit in his mother's eyes? You stranger, in your deafness, filled with rotten mandrake roots. . . ." And sometimes she'd even clench her fists.

And then Mort would lower his great big palm down on her thigh and look sympathetic. He, too, knew what it was to be a stranger in another's land. Once, in one of her moods, he'd suggested she take a Great Books course. It would give her insight into her problems, he said.

"Big stupid Jew," she said under her breath, "piss on

your Israel. For two years I worked like a pack animal. Don't tell *me* about Mother Israel."

With them it was different, they were born to it, these stevedore kibbutz women, with their hair under their armpits longer than Hassidic earlocks . . . lifting and toting to them wasn't such a deal. "But you didn't care. You weren't pregnant!"

"Shhhh," Mort would cry. "He'll hear you. Our son, asleep, the little rabbit, in the other room."

"Our *Jewish* son, you mean. What about me? America, for instance, where, instead of with you, I could be living like my sister Paula. Summers in Switzerland. A maid and twelve rooms on Park Avenue. Paintings under glass. Paintings not under glass. I should have listened to Mother; at least, among her many other excesses, she'd so far avoided marriage to a son of Abraham. If Sabra is so wonderful, why did you have to come looking in the social register? Some promised land. Won't you admit that your own son had rickets?

"You think my sister walked to the delivery room? Put her own feet in two tin cans strapped to the side of an old door and leaned over to pull out her own first born like any long-haired mongrel? At least when I was raging with fever they could have let me stop nursing the baby."

"Frontier conditions do not come in even sizes, Ashley. You knew there would be sacrifices."

"I hate you," she said. "I hate the feel of your Brillo chest and your sandpaper cheek. I hate the day I happened to hold your hand in my first hora and looked up to find a partner I couldn't let go of when it came time for the hambo."

Mort thought it was funny. Funny, her cheekbones, her skin, the way her hair hung down straight. So different from the big, soft girls he went to Midwood High School with. He would have figured a girl like Ashley, a tennis player, a girl who could swim across the country club pool a hundred times would have taken to frontier life like a native.

Genero Mendola stopped his pickup at the corner of Elm and Central, so nobody would see Ashley get out. Then, barely waiting for her to close the door, he took off for The Zork Hardware Company of New Mexico so he could pick up the piece for the wringer on his mother's washer. He didn't say anything to her as he left, but then he never did. She just knew that one afternoon he'd come around and she'd be waiting. After all . . . he needed her.

She knocked very quietly on Lester's door and then took a few steps backward as the two men yelled at each other. The one with the freckles was trying to explain to the other one how the Hebrew blood came to be all over their Tlingit wall hanging, and then she saw Mort sleeping it off on the floor.

"What happened?" she asked them, but as they didn't pay any attention to her, she just came in and got down on her hands and knees to see if she couldn't find Mort's glasses before she dragged him out to the car.

· 15 ·

got or gave, heads or tails, he shuddered with an ecstasy of guilt. No matter how good the feel, he would still have to atone. A broken bone, another enervating disease. You give, that's all, especially this time. This time he was in for something bone-crunching.

"Didn't I tell you a hundred times . . ."

"You told me."

"A hundred times without fail. On top of everything else, I said, 'Lester, this is madness.' "

"If I had only known."

While he was on his knees, later on his fat belly. On his ass, "Didn't I say, Lester . . . Lester, don't we have a good life, you and I? Lester, what are you looking

· 104 ·

for, with this band conductor? Lester, who needs it?"

"You told me. Yes, you told me. . . . You were right. Ron, flat on my back? Ron, you on top of me? How, Ron, do it first. You can yell later. . . ."

But later it was Ron's turn to listen. As he lay on his back, all sweaty on the sandy down of his ass. He'd won over Lester's old girlfriend, Joyce, and now, or whenever it suited him, he could drag out Lester's latest blunder and rub it in or down his throat, at will. He could also make Lester tell him what he wanted to hear. And right now it was about the great conquest. He always wanted to hear about that.

He picked Lester's hand off the chenille and lay it on top of the belt. He took an index finger and traced it around the smooth silver conchos. Along with Ron's pleasure in winning, he liked to possess. Belts, fidelity, and total submissiveness on the part of his possessions.

"Again," he said and closed his eyes. The peace of the sleeping cat furred down the back of his neck. The beaten pieces of silver eights spoked around his fat waist like a rock path around the Continental Divide. Ron worshipped the belt because he owned it. Because he'd made up his mind and won. Like he'd win over Lester's desire not to tell the story of the belt's conquest again, because he didn't like to be reminded of it.

"Go on, you owe me."

Lester looked down at the spider's web turquoise veins through the oval stones and saw the bloodshot eyes in the old man's face.

"O.K., O.K.," he said and thought back. To the time Ron made up his mind. To Thanksgiving when Ron had come for a visit and decided to stay for good. They had driven to Gallop for a day's bargains and were deciding whether or not to continue on to Zuni for the Shalako because it was so cold. It would be so late when they got back. They weren't really dressed for it. Everything was so much more expensive than they'd anticipated and then they saw him, this beat-up Indian, a hundred and ten, with a face like a snow tire. He was wearing sneakers, a pink and blue Montgomery Ward blanket and a fortune in pawn jewelry. But from the first it was the belt. So heavy with coin silver and finely matched turquoise, it pulled down the Indian's greasy pants under his brown belly. He was also wearing two squashes, six strings of dirty wampum, one of matched coral, five sandcasts, and a ring on every finger including his thumbs. He was leaning against a telephone pole on the highway, just before the left turn to Zuni and Ron wanted that belt.

He nudged Lester and they pulled over. The old guy himself said it was worth more than all the rest put together and was so heavy it gave him a red welt under his pants. He even showed them the welt. The color in the turquoise glowed with the transparency of a Chartres window and the old man let them hold it under the streetlight.

He told them it had been made by his grandmother and had won first prize in the state fair at Santa Fe. He admitted being able to wear it only a few hours a year. For the Shalako. Christmas Day, if all went well, after which it went back into pawn along with all the rest of his estate. He invited them home, promised them a seat of honor, and a fistful of his wife's parchment-thin bread. He even said a grandson would sit on their laps, but he laughed when they said, "sell." He threw his turtle's head back and showed a lot of purple gum. He said he'd sooner give up his nineteen-inch Admiral with his wife thrown in. . . . Even when they offered seventy-five dollars, enough to keep him in sandcasts round the clock. He shook his head and said it was very good, very good. And he laughed some more but he wouldn't sell.

It got darker. The men rushed by in their pickups. The Indian didn't move. He just stood there and laughed that fuck-you laugh of a man a hundred and ten if he was a day, who didn't care if you stood on your prick.

So when Ron moved to the west for good and Lester had it, all gift wrapped and waiting, it had become the rosetta stone of their love. He'd never taken it off and the leather was all curled around the edges and had left a dye line around his belly like a tub ring.

Ron Harkness, Ph.D., was a happy man. Just a week before, in the men's room at the Placitas Place, he'd run into a bigwig from the psych department at the university, lady luck. There, Ron on his knees, the man's trousers down around his ankles. It turned out the man was in a position to refer more business Ron's way than he could shake his middle finger at. Ron had his shingle. Ron had Lester. Ron had his belt. "I'm waiting," he said, fiddling around with Lester's ear lobe. "Tell me again how he looked when you got it."

"I was reading," Lester said. "I was reading and along came Chess Hoffer . . . Why do I have to tell you every day, all day?"

"Chess Hoffer came and then what?"

"And then . . . and then he said do I want to go gouging?" Lester's stomach started hurting under his chest. It felt like a fire but he knew what it was. He coated it with two Saltines and a glass of milk. "Do I want to go gouging? I said, what's that? And what's the difference, you got it."

It turned out "gouging" was a private word for Indian trading. Trading with secondhand kids' clothes picked up at Goodwill for two cents on a dollar, and with which a smart operator could come away with a hundred concho belts.

Lester hadn't intended telling Ron right from the start, but Ron had a way of getting what he wanted. And at first he told him as he looked in the other direction, but after four months he'd gotten a little more used to it. He ran his fingertips up and down his lover's leg and told how he'd gone and bought three overwashed sweaters with long stretched-out arms, a snowsuit size 6X, rubber boots, and a striped stocking cap and then four pairs of corduroy overalls just to make sure. How he'd driven to Gallop with Chess and found the same goddamn Indian, only this time the only thing he was still wearing that Lester recognized was the pink and blue Montgomery Ward blanket.

"Christ." He looked away.

"Christ?"

"O.K., I held up a couple of moth-eaten sweaters, a size 4 snowsuit, and a Flexible Flyer that could only steer to the right."

"And he jumped."

"Yeah, he jumped all right."

He could hardly wait to get to the trading post, the grocery, hardware, haberdashery pawnshop trading post where he and the rest of them had their family jewels all tied up in pawn tickets and IOUs.

"But what the hell," he said. "If I didn't, Chess Hoffer, or some other gouger would have come along, right?" Ron didn't say anything. "O.K., so I let him. I gave him all that shit and that was that. He traded me the belt, that's all.

"It's not funny," Lester said, but Ron kept on laughing. He had his hand on his belt and was shaking his head the way he always shook it every single time Lester told him.

"Are you going to listen to me, next time?" he said, then, suddenly lifting his head up and squeezing Lester's shoulder. "Are you going to do what I tell you and stay home and keep out of trouble?"

"I'm going to listen to you," Lester told him.

"Do you love me?"

But instead of waiting for an answer, Ron just rolled him over, jammed it in, and did it again.

· 16 ·

ever it was hung up. Dave Collins sat next to the phone and let it jar his nerves rather than pick it up and find out what Trini Lucero, God forbid, wanted.

"Stop shaking, for godsakes."

"I am not shaking."

"Oh, but you are, David dear," his wife said, buttering her toast. "You are shaking as if the mean old Ronald Croonquist were hiding under your egg cup again. What are you afraid of, that he's going to bite off your beautiful handmade nose right through the telephone wires?"

"Don't be cute."

"I thought that's why you found me so irresistible. . . ." Then she leaned forward and hissed, "There must be some reason why you put up with me . . . I sure as hell wouldn't."

He let his head fall into his hands and she said he looked like a bull just after the picadors had severed its neck muscles. . . . "My hero," she crooned.

"Don't you realize what association with a known Commu——"

"Oh, Jesus, David. Why don't you make one clean gesture of patriotism and get it over with. Paint a hand grenade red, white and blue, stick it up your giggy, and blow yourself up. That ought to show your good faith."

Now that really made Dave mad, but when he got up to give it to her good, she'd already gone into the other room. In all their married life, even in the army, he'd never gotten through to her what it was like to be followed by your own government. If he was suspect once, he could be suspect twice. So it simply wasn't as simple as losing his job . . . did she really think that was all that was bothering him? For god-sakes . . . he'd already peed in Joe McCarthy's face. She simply did not understand all the ramifications. . . . And for his sake he hoped she never would. He sighed.

· 17 ·

AFTER SETTING THE CHARRED
corpse of his father's cat under his father's pillow, Jack
Samuels thought of yet another way to wish his father
farewell before taking off for New Mexico for good.

"Relax," his father had warned him before leaving
for the evening. "Relax!" Which, meant: "Don't screw
up kid, I'm warning you!!" But dinner and the theater
also meant that Jack had plenty of time to hit and still
run before his dad got home to check up on him.
Daddy, Martin W., President, founder, and bulwark
of Acme, Acme, Acme, and Samuels, producers and dis-
tributors of Acmes and Samuels, Ltd., Inc. What does
the kid think? Even a bulwark can't go on forever!!!

The kid. The liability would be more like it. The

constant drain on the wallet, with sanatoriums, head shrinkers, and tranquilizers, not that any of them, the goddamn experts, knew what the hell any of them were talking about. The kid was swell, the kid was O.K., wouldn't a father know? The kid's goddamn father, for godsakes? Martin W., who was married to a dependent clause, ruled both family and empire with the same divine right. Alice Samuels, Jack's mother, had had a smile sewn into place twenty years ago and had never since been told to remove it. She had also been told that if she spoke when spoken to, her husband would consider her contribution to their relationship more than sufficient, and that beyond an occasional interjection nothing more would ever be required of her.

She seemed quite early on to have adjusted.

Being married and producing a dynasty were necessities for successful empire-building and Martin W. Samuels very early in life knew what he wanted. He not only kept a wife and a descendant around the house, but two dog-eating pit bulls, who had once, in a successful joint rampage, gotten the taste of coonhound jugular and never forgot it.

Jack had always been afraid of him, and them. Couldn't remember a moment ever when he hadn't been. Even back before Menninger, he could remember hours of terror behind the chintz chaise in his mother's bedroom sucking on the ends of the long red tassles that hung from the bottom. Jack had been almost eight before even attempting baby talk and even after four years away in Kansas, going home on vacation for two days was enough to throw him into one of his states, sucking on doorknobs, peeing on the rugs, and playing with what his mother called his member.

"Did Momma's baby make a touch-touch?" she once asked him, and his father thundered from the next room that if he ever heard her gah-gah again he'd crack both their skulls open.

"Get your goddamn hands out of your goddamn zipper or I'll tear it out by the roots!" he bellowed. Not that he was always threatening. Sometimes he handed out lollipops, except that he had a way of making "Let's go to the zoo," scary.

"Naturally you're good-looking!" he'd rave. "You're *my* son!" Like, God help you if you raised a pimple.

All Jack had to do was smell his father's aftershave to break into raw sores up and down his arms. "What do you think? I built a goddamn sporting-goods empire for my own goddamn pleasure? From a penny-ante sweatsock operation for nobody? For you, goddamn you! For my one and only heir who sits there pissing on my goddamn Oriental rugs! Take that goddamn little Tinker-Toy of yours out of your goddamn hands—you're going to need those hands to take the wheel! Stick it where it'll do the name of Samuels some goddamn good, you goddamn little pissant," he screamed, even though he paid first Dr. Klein, then Drs. Goldenberger, Brigham, Heinrich, and Gershorn to tell him that perhaps there was a better approach to Jack's problem. "Shove his problems," he'd bellow. "Who's the goddamn captain of this goddamn ship?"

Well, the captain was out and Jack moved. First he cooked his father's cat. Then he switched on every light in the house. Next to Angela, his father prized economy. Nothing reamed his father's ass more than wasting electricity, so only when Jack had the place lit up like a beacon could he carry on, pick up the old man's hand-carved andirons, and whack away at the old man's genuine imported chandelier.

"Fore!" he shouted, "Fore!" swung, and then backed up to watch two, four, six, eight, a hundred prisms fall to the blue Bokhara. Then, with his father's own hobnailed bowling shoes, Jack ground each rainbow into powdered splinters. And on into the kitchen.

The kitchen had been his mother's one and only bone of contention. The kitchen was her domain, she had argued, the center of her world even, which impressed his father about as much as his wedding vows. "Please," she had begged him, "please let me keep the brick floor, the cast-iron pots, and the beautiful, hand-rubbed cherry tables."

"Keep, my ass," Jack's father told Jack's mother. "Be satisfied I let you crap up the rest of the place. You and your Tiffany, Regency, Linsey-woolsey, carnival bric-a-brac. Piss on your brick floor, cast-iron pots, and the rest of your horse shit." Whereupon, Martin W. proceeded to build his wife a kitchen he could be proud of. Money no object. The newest, finest, shiniest, most Formicaed kitchen in the neighborhood. Chock-full of every modern miracle.

First Jack disassembled the Kitchen Aid, found a Kotex, mopped up some of Angela's bowels with it, and then shoved same down the Insinkerator. He poured lingonberries down the automatic General

Electric toaster and Drambuie into the Amana double exhaust pipe fridge. He unplugged the handle of the electric frying pan, where it said "Do not immerse in water," and cooked it to a rolling boil with three bottles of Taittinger '49. Then, when it was ready, he floated the Grundig portable and the RCA speaker for the hi-fi in it. He stapled filet mignons to the back of the recessed lights where, when they began to thaw, the blood would seep into the connections. He caulked the stove burners with imported Dijon. He pissed into the eggplant antipasto and ground anchovies into the works of the blender. But it wasn't until he disconnected the freezer that he really got into the swing of things. Disconnected it and threw over both shoulders: shell steaks, Alaskan crab, squab, capon, and small, well-trimmed lamb chops into a big pile in the middle of his father's hand-laid, handsome ceramic tile floor, until he'd made a great big pile of frozen packages, all wrapped in white paper and labeled with the fast Ms and brutal Ts of his beloved father.

Only then, red-cheeked and bright-eyed, did he call for a cab, double-lock the front door, and run away from home; but not before leaving his father the tape he had made recording the execution of Angela the cat. He left this in lieu of a farewell note, but he did leave his old *Mother Goose Rhymes* opened to page 113, where it said:

> I love little Pussy,
> Her coat is so warm;
> And if I don't hurt her
> She'll do me no harm. . . .

· 18 ·

BOTH TRINI AND HIS ROOM-
mate, Cremencio Ortega, had skins like toads. A lot of
people took them for twins, especially because they'd
been together since college, but it was nothing like that.
It was just that girls were hard. Mostly they settled for
chocolate milk with dinner.

The week after the special meeting of the Board of
Education, Cremencio left work early in order to have
Trini's favorite dinner on the table when he got home
(chicken à la king, with banana creme pie for dessert).
Cremencio repossessed cars for Dallas Motors. He even
picked up a small box of malt to go with the Nestlés
because of the solemnity of the occasion, only it wasn't
till everything was overdone and a thick rubbery skin

had formed on the top of the creamed chicken that he realized Trini had been home all along.

"I know," he said, sitting down on the chair next to Trini's bed, but that's all. What could he say? His hands were heavy in his lap and his suitcase was already packed. Trini nodded and lay with his arms at his sides. Under the circumstances, they both knew it was the only possible decision, but they also knew who would answer Trini's ad: ROOM FOR LET. LANDLORD: PUBLIC ENEMY NÚMERO UNO.

Quien sabe?

Cremencio played double bass. He and Trini always meant to play music together, but it had been hard. Even if they transposed, the range of an oboe and a double bass didn't take in a very wide repertoire. Still, in the darkened bedroom, even with the shades drawn, Trini could tell there were tears on Cremencio's cheeks.

Then Trini got lucky, or thought he did. He wrote out another ad, changed his name, and in three days had the room rented to a fellow named Jack Samuels who always wore a ski sweater and seemed very nice.

· 19 ·

JACK SAMUELS MOVED INTO
his new room as the old tenant moved out. He didn't
like the idea of living in spic town, but having just lost
his job when Valley Gold discovered him spitting into
the cottage cheese, what alternatives did he have? He
couldn't go on showering at the fags'—they were getting suspicious. Plus which, he'd met two different
whores in the last week who both needed a place to do
it in.

But the room turned out to have its advantages. The
landloard called himself Velásquez, but whenever Jack
called him by name, he seemed surprised. As if he
weren't quite sure that was who he was. Something

funny all right . . . something Jack was hoping would turn into something interesting.

But all in all, counting the panty raids, the sudden car crashes, and especially that girl, the one he'd taken to spying on at night, New Mexico agreed with him. He could even see himself settling down, getting himself an adobe, and maybe even a wife and a couple of kids.

· 20 ·

the panty raid, Amy developed a cankersore. She
climbed into her own bed in her own room and put
her head under her pillow. The cankersore was between
her legs and her mother called the doctor who said in a
German accent that the adolescent reaction to precoital
anxiety often brought on the symptoms of pseudoshock,
why didn't they bring her in for a diaphragm fitting; he
could fit her on Thursday.

Dell got Dave—"My little girl, a diaphragm?"—to
pry their eldest out of bed and together they held her
legs apart long enough for the doctor to write out a
prescription for a size 75 Ortho. It took Dave months to
get over the shock. He took to long walks with Ron

Croonquist. Often out on the mesa, where they could be alone, so that Saturday, when Dell was off on one of what she called her "assignations," Amy was alone in the house. She wouldn't let anybody take her Ortho out after Dr. Mueller put it in. It even took Dr. Mueller a half hour to get her to let him take his hand out. And now she just walked around the house waiting.

The doorbell rang and she was ready. Trini Lucero, out on the doorstep, was desperate. If nobody would answer the phone, there was more than one way to smoke out a shy Legislative Guild Representative.

"Open up, I can hear you panting," he said, tapping his nails against the pane in the door. She was looking at all his teeth. So what? she said to herself. You're not exactly going to stick your head in the gift horse's mouth. She went to the door and Trini burst out, "I have to tell somebody. You don't understand. This Mort Dralon affair has been a nightmare."

"Morton Milton Dralon," he moaned. "No matter what I do. . . . Him and his petition. His Trinidad Lucero Defense Committee. . . . Who said *Save Lucero?* Trini Lucero will never want to be saved." She stroked his arm. She felt the rim of her size 75 Ortho press against her brain. She listened to him tell her how important it was he speak to the Legislative Guild Representative before they added sedition to his other sins. And she thought if she told him her father had only taken the job because her mother had said it would get them to the Convention of State Educators where she might run into a whole new crop of cocksmen, it might have slowed him down a little. Stopped the flow of saliva down the front of his double-breasted stomach.

"What's it amount to?" her mother had said to her father. "Gowan, take it."

Her father said to her mother, "I'll tell you what it amounts to. It amounts to up-setting the equilibrium, I don't know what it amounts to. It amounts to all manner of unknown territories. I don't want to," he'd begged her. But her mother had won in the end. He was crowned Legislative Guild Representative in spite of himself, and Trinidad Lucero clasped the front of Amy's robe, tears rolling down his cheeks.

"I don't even know Mort Dralon," Trini moaned, "I only met him once. One time. You've got to help me. I can't call anymore. My index finger's a nervous wreck. I tell you I can't take much more of this."

He shifted his weight from one blue-serge leg to the other, still holding the front of her robe, and she figured if she moved a little sideways and a little back, by the time she got him inside the door he would forget the reluctant representative.

"Cigarette?" she said, sidling.

"Don't smoke."

"A drink maybe?"

A quiet, "No, thank you," and before he had a chance to wring a hand or say another word about what the Board of Education thought about anything, she'd taken a sudden jerk, her robe was open, and her black pubes and spongy soft chi-chis were hanging there square in his face, which he didn't want either.

"*Hijo de puta,*" he murmured and thought to himself, don't I have enough heartache?

"Gotcha!" She screamed and leaped at the same time. At blue-serge him, who'd do in the pinch she was in. She wrapped herself around him like clothesline and she sucked away at his marrow, lover! Oh lover, now was the moment! Not that Trini was altogether inexperienced when it came to girls. When he was a junior at Southern Catholic, he'd had a girl. Named Bea, who played bassoon. Only his father had said, "What do you need her for? She hasn't even *got* anything," holding his hands out in front of his chest, palms upward, to squeeze the air.

"Miss! Please, Miss Collins," and it occurred to him again, now that he couldn't run from it. . . . It occurred to him that it was strange, his father's knowing that, about Bea, his bassoonist, who always wore a stiff white gym blouse. The kind with the starch so thick you could get a paper cut!

Amy Collins worked till in between a bicuspid and four extra incisors she found enough space to stick her tongue. Well, it wasn't her beautiful blond almost-rapist, but it was something, and Amy Collins was pushing eighteen. She propped an index finger back at his bite so he couldn't close his jaw on her tongue.

"Cooperate," she told him, but he shook his head because he thought, with her tongue in his mouth, that she had said, "Be a good skate," and why should he?

"You don't understand, Miss Collins."

"Sure I do," she hollered. "You're the one who keeps calling, and you've got a little time and you're waiting and . . . and open up," she said nuzzling, rubbing herself all around, all around, all at the same time.

He tried to wiggle out from under but wiggling was what he had to avoid. He tried to push her but the strength of her grip was incredible. A lamp fell off the table next to the chair and she didn't care if school kept or not. She had her eyes closed and as he pulled and writhed she saw Billy Dawson. She saw Billy Dawson in his picture as Rookie of the Year, the one she'd ripped from the yearbook and kept under her pillow. Billy Dawson, as he looked just before jumping out her window at the Hall of the Virgin Butterflies.

Trini's lower bowel rumbled like a tiny boat in a big ocean and he panicked. "Not now," he moaned, and Amy thought he meant her. "You bet, now," she answered, and tore at his fly with her toes because everything else was busy.

Trini read once in a dentist's office that it was the smell of women that drove men wild, so he held his breath. Nothing on earth would make him smell this girl from the *nice* family, who was sticking out downthere tongues as slippery as pimientos. And he concentrated on not feeling the familiar rumbling in the bottom layer of his guts.

Amy was prying his mouth open, tearing at him, a skinny hen at the evening corn, frantically. . . . Her size 75 Ortho tight as a fist up her giggy.

His teeth, his ears, his *thing*! This *nice* girl? Whose father, the Legislative Guild Representative, held the key to his kingdom next to his humidor stuffed with old apples. "My God, my God," Trini moaned. . . . And how was it that so many worlds could crumble all at the same time? Mort Dralon on his back, Amy Collins in his pants.

He fought valiantly, one hand over his tassle, the other against her (chest in between), not touching. Her chi-chis. Her plopping, smacking chi-chis back and forth against the backs of hands, God help him. And all the while the rumbling. That constant, turning, churning rumbling that thwumped around down there telling him, Watch out, big boy, you're in real trouble now!

He held and he held but finally, when she pushed and wiggled at once, making it impossible to keep a respectful distance, when he could feel *it*, that dirty, awful *it* in his own pants push up like a jack-in-the-box, he could control himself no longer, He farted. And loud.

"Excuse me," he said. "I'm sorry."

"Sure."

"I didn't mean it," and he farted again.

But she bit into his chin, which tasted better than bacon rind, and he could keep it up all day as far as she was concerned.

"No!" he moaned. And again she thought he meant her and let go of his chin. Which was when he felt his first sphincter spasm. And soon after the first another and more—one lightning shot after another until finally his whole body pulled itself up off the chair and exploded!

Peeyooo.

There was a great brown shitball that had traveled down an endless cellular roller coaster . . . down a small intestine into a large one. Six farts and then out it went through the sphincter onto his shorts. And Trini knew it was coming. Whenever he got into a situation he couldn't handle, he made in his pants, and had ever since he was a kid.

At first all she knew was the smell. And then came the tears, pouring out just before she was flung off his lap onto her back, where she flailed around like a capsized turtle.

He ran for the john, wiping his hands up and down on his pants as if that would help. Too late, again too late, always too late, as usual. . . .

Amy could hear the noises through the bathroom door. And afterwards, Trini desperately cutting his shorts into little inconspicuous shreds with nail clippers he found in the medicine chest. Then the rummaging in the wastebasket where he hid each piece separately so nobody would know. When he came back into the room, the girl was rocking back and forth on the floor like a hobbyhorse. When her body swung forward, her head would crack against her knees quite hard. She wasn't making a sound but he could tell by the enlarged veins on the sides of her neck that she was screaming somewhere.

Trini didn't know what to do. If he left now, how could he come back? How would he ever be able to start his explanations up the chain of command all the way to the Board of Education? About petitions with his name at the top and signatures at the bottom. About the beauty of fulfilled guilt . . . the inner peace he had been prepared to bathe in until the advent of the Committee to Save Trinidad Lucero.

When he had straightened his jacket and looked around to make sure there was nothing left on the chair next to the humidor with the smell of apple, the girl had gotten up and was standing next to the mirror combing her hair. Who would have imagined such unusual behavior, he thought. From a nice girl like her?

Her robe was closed and she was wiping off a loose eyelash with the end of her pinkie. Finally he said very quietly, "You know, miss. . . . You just can't go around doing things like that." Amy laughed.

She turned around and looked him straight in the face and said, "Apparently not."

After he was gone, she stood there, in the same spot in front of the mirror, and threw her arms up into the air. Then she screamed out loud just as loud as she could. "Apparently, it was just not done," she said to her reflection. "Apparently that was not the way to go about it either."

· 21 ·

THE BLOOD HAD DRIED ON Mort's wounds. So far he knew from nothing about Genero Mendola. His math class did, outside of shredding all the texts into spitballs, nothing to him that week, and nobody he knew had a cold, but that didn't mean Mort's mind was at ease. He was, in fact, consumed with anguish, for the question of whether or not to continue his defense of Trinidad Lucero haunted his every hour. It had become a moral dilemma and on the one horn was the question of the unalienable rights. But, on the other horn was Trini Lucero himself, and was this Mexican-American, America Firster, any better than Heil Hitler?

The conflict was reaching crisis proportions. On the

slide rule, it came to 3.7 hours of sleep per night he was
losing on account of it. How long could he endure this
torture, he asked himself. The answer seemed to be he
could take anything he was willing to dish out. Until
one night at 4:09 P.M. he woke with a start. His path
was clear. The underdog, never mind its bark, was still
the underdog. After he defended his right to rights,
there'd be plenty of time to blacken his eye. He felt
immediate relief and woke Ashley up so he could
spread her legs and share his decision with her. He
could hardly wait for daybreak to call Trinidad Lucero
and reassure him. Mort was a new man. Trini, though
he was glad to hear that, began to worry even more
intensely. He took out Billy Dawson's address and
looked at it. He weighed the consequences of calling on
him and his good right arm. He added up the repercussions and subtracted the anxiety. He checked his answers by casting out nines, but it wasn't until Mort, in
the privacy of his own soul, decided to shelve the Trinidad Lucero Defense Committee altogether (because of
Ashley's practically losing his seed) and forgot to inform Trini that Trini decided he had no other choice.
Had Mort remembered, in his panic, to call Trini . . .
had he told him, "Gee, I'm sorry fellah, I don't mean to
let you down, but you know how it is . . . ," that
would have been the end of that. But he didn't, so
Trini called Billy. An entirely new set of plans were set
into motion and nobody's left hands had any idea of
what their rights were up to.

Certainly not Mort, who had become in the last two
days consumed with the high treason his wife had per-

petrated upon him. For, as Mort put it, with such poign-ancy, "What does it gainest a man to inherit the wind, if he losest his own seed?"

It happened, he remembered, after school when Mort was taking the family up behind the village to see the pictographs and the petroglyphs, though the difference between the two was, even to him, a bit murky. He had the boy's hand in his, and was pointing up to a rash of drawings scratched like a sort of city sidewalk standing up on the side of the mountain. "There," he told him, "look!" But the little boy saw nothing. He became quite desperate, his eyes running back and forth over the cliff wall like scalded ants. But sensing something he couldn't quite identify, something else, it became crucial that he at least see the "pricta-drifts." "Where?" he screamed. "Where?" while his father held up his chin and again directed his eye and finally, just before the hysterics, lined up his vision so the little boy could read the old Indian messages drawn on the cliff the way he himself used to see

Jane Sucks
BU 4-6879

on the subway walls.

A ways off, resting her belly against a rock, Ashley spent her time peering out over the valley for a glimpse of Genero Mendola. She once thought she saw him go to her back door and then leave again and hoped the boy would quickly find something up there, some piece of Indian pot. Anything. So they could call it a day and go home. She watched them, her husband and son, as familiar as Big and Little Klaus, no more, and wrote with her finger in the sand; *GM* for Genero Mendola, loves *AD*, for Ashley Dralon. It somehow gave her a sense of enormous grandeur, even though the truth was he'd only stuck it in her maybe eleven times. Sometimes she almost had to coax him.

In a way, her lover reminded her of a dog. A desert dog that doesn't seem to belong to anybody, the way he sucked not so much spit as what might have been spit, back and forth, in and out of his mouth. He'd said later that their first time had been a bet, even though she didn't believe him. "Why should anybody bet anybody else such a thing?" she said, and it also occurred to her that that first time she might have screamed, or at least have told him to get out this minute. Only she didn't. She just watched him come across the room and lean against her Guatemalan skirt with his jeans. He was always covered with a fine layer of gray dust. And she could feel the palms of his hands that always seemed to remind her of cow patties. Stiff, as if they'd been lying on the mesa, out in the sun, a long, long time.

She smiled to herself because Mort still didn't know about him. And wouldn't even after she lost the baby. Why should he? It was none of the man's business if the woman wanted her freedom!

"Ashley," Mort said suddenly. She turned and he said, "The child isn't wearing any socks."

"That's funny," she said. "It's cold out. He should be wearing socks," but she turned back again. Maybe Genero would come out again. Maybe he was even wondering where she was. She then felt a sudden tightening in her stomach and wondered nervously if that was it. But it went away again, right off, so she drew a heart in the dirt and pierced it with an arrow.

"You dig too," the child was screeching. He was hitting the side of Mort's legs. His face was puckered up like a pomegranate. It occurred to Ashley that the boy might miss his father after she'd gone. Because the truth was he was good with him. She had to admit that.

The boy kept on screaming until Mort knelt distractedly by his side and picked up a stick. The wind blew and it was chilly. "Yes," he said softly, "Daddy dig too." Then he carelessly hit the side of his head very lightly, with the flat of his palm, to stop the echos of the boy's screaming. The boy sneezed.

"Gee, Ashley," he said. "I don't understand how you could forget socks on a day like today."

Ashley felt a second pain. Vaguely familiar. A little bit like a middle of the month pain. A little bit like one she couldn't put her finger on, but it soon went away. She buttoned her jacket. She heard what Mort said but couldn't quite separate the words. So she nodded her head and stared off over the valley again. It was the eighth time she had buttoned her jacket in the past half-hour. Between the blaze of the sun and the cold wind, it was hard to strike an easy medium. She shifted her weight to the other hip.

Mort said, "Gee whiz, it sure was a beautiful day." Rhile said, "Dig!" Ashley shifted her weight back again. The load of the pregnancy was getting to the uncomfortable stage. Her back ached. She couldn't seem to get settled. Mort was still, in his innocence, thinking about Trini Lucero. He'd decided to bring a knockwurst with him when he went. They should sit around and get to know one another.

"After all," he murmured to himself, "isn't that just what America's strength is? The harmonious concentration of differences of opinion?" He would save Trini in spite of all. He was sure of it.

"What?" Ashley said. But before Mort could say, "Nothing," her face was suddenly screwed up like a Samurai on the attack. She wrenched herself in half as if somebody had socked her in the belly button.

"What is it? Ashley?" He jumped towards her, ready. But Ashley, warding off his inevitable embrace, crumpled like a used Kleenex. He backed off. He sat on his haunches, immobile, as one pain after another ran over his wife's body, as finally, the child, terrorized, threw himself on her back and dug his dirty fingers into her.

"It's all right," she moaned. She panted, grabbing air between pains. "I'm having a miscarriage." Mort picked Rhile off like a peppercorn from a slice of pastrami. "A miscarriage?" he said. "*Vus vilstu* a miscarriage?" When in real life she'd driven into Gallup for a small medicine bottle and a lot of promises. He lay his head on her belly as if it were a stethoscope, and that was the end of Trini Lucero. "Oh my gosh!" he moaned, how could he have been so selfish . . . ? What husband and father worth his candle could care a fig for unalienable rights at a time like that?

· 134 ·

"You're heavy," Ashley said and he pulled back his head. The child crouched and watched.

How could that be, a miscarriage? She never had a miscarriage before. The little boy said, "What is Mommy having?"

Mort said, "A rest. She's having a rest."

"No," he said, stubbornly. He banged his foot on the edge of the cliff. "She said she was having something. What did she say she was having?"

"Why don't you go dig for your genuine Indian whistle?" Mort said, and again Ashley rolled into a little ball and quivered like a used-up slingshot. She laid her hands flat on her belly and inside felt a waterfall. Mort spit on a hanky and wiped the dirt from her face. The smell of his spit made her squint. "She is," the boy said. He was socking his father as hard as he could. "She is, too, having something. . . ." And then Ashley said maybe she should go to a hospital. Her voice was even, the same as when she told Rhile about Maeterlinck's bees, or what Mort should bring from the grocery, a sack of lentils, a box of safety matches.

"Or at least the midwife," she whispered and Mort couldn't stop pacing. The hospital? A miscarriage? His poor defenseless seed? Of course she should go to a hospital. Nothing was too good for his wife and seed. But why a miscarriage? A woman out to there, with good, wide hips and an ample tunnel? He looked at the fruit of his first seed. The seed who had . . . and she moaned and wound her body as tight as a golf ball from pain.

The doctor had charged her ten dollars and promised that the remedy had been handed down from Zuni witchdoctor to Zuni witchdoctor. Genero Mendola had driven her over in the pickup. She told him it was for in-grown toenails because men didn't like to get involved. So it was silly to think they'd make it to the hospital. She began to be worried. The pains hit harder. Why, she wondered, were they always in the middle of some desert a whole generation removed from a doctor?

"I'll carry you," he said, "down the cliff. . . ."

She screamed. . . . "No," she screamed, "I can feel it," and where was Trini Lucero then? And who cared?

"She can feel it, Daddy. What can she feel?"

"Don't move me," she begged, in a quick, grunting voice like an old dog, then she was still. Nobody moved. Only Ashley, trying to fold her legs in some magic way that would make it all comfortable. She hadn't remembered Rhile's coming as that hard. In the middle of the Negev, while Mort was out threshing the waving Israeli wheat, or whatever he was doing to it. . . . Another pain.

"Go dig," Mort said, and the child nodded his head and made little scooping motions with his other hand.

Ashley wriggled out of her skirt and Mort called her the salt of the earth.

She said he shouldn't take it so hard, it was only a fetus, and the blue stretch marks on her belly pulled tense and white. She was lying in a pool of rocky sweat and then, imperceptibly, the quality of the pain changed. It was a little like expecting the second wind that never shows up. She knew immediately that it was all over. The peak had come and gone, and she could kick herself for believing a bottle of sour brew from a quack doctor in the middle of no place could put a halt to anything Mort Dralon had started.

She started to cry. Quietly at first and then a lot. Mort couldn't bear it. He reached down and a minute later was running back and forth like a rabid fox with her in his arms . . . first here and then the other way. "Stop," she screamed, but their broken connection jangled on. From far away she could hear the little boy sing "The Farmer in the Dell." Before they sank to the earth in that tenuous moment between kneeling and finished, she knew she had been had. Here she was and here she would be, with her belly out to there, and Mort and the boy and nothing else forever. She covered the both of them with a false rush of dark spots, but without looking she knew there would be no blackening clots or lumps. No tiny withered form, all turned in on itself with thread-thin flippers and a head that was all forehead the size of a poppyseed roll.

They lay for a while in stillness and she realized that the tune was "The Farmer in the Dell" but the words were different. Mort held her and mourned for the seed that still grew inside like goldenrod and Rhile started in on his third chorus.

> My mommy's going to die!
> My mommy's going to die!
> Heigh-ho, the derry-ooo,
> My mommy's going to die!!!

· 22 ·

SINCE IT WAS ALWAYS DARK
and he always disappeared into a shadow the minute
she got close enough for a good look, Amy couldn't be
sure. But it looked like him. The guy in the orange ski
sweater, from the panty raid. Who, she was sure, had
meant business. It got so it didn't matter where she
went, sooner or later she'd feel those hot eyes of his, up
her leg like a daddy longlegs. She only wished he
wouldn't run off like he did; ready as she was for a
Dial-A-Screw service. Anything to get rid of that constant gnawing in her underwear.

She even took to walking down alleys. Two nights in
a row she took overnights just to hang around First
Street. But with her luck it rained both nights. And it

never rained in New Mexico. The only one who followed her was him, and when she stopped, so did he. When she'd turn around, all she got was his afterimage. She was going nuts, the screaming meemies, full speed ahead, down there between her legs.

"Come and get me," she screamed, but still nothing happened. Until the morning it came in the mail. A little white envelope with a sheet of three-holed loose-leaf paper inside. It said:

> We shall meet again, you and I.
> There is a bond between us.

Very nice, but where did it get her? If it was supposed to be so easy to become a loose woman, how come it turned out to be so hard?

The next note was on the same paper and said:

> I know your movements,
> when you come in or go out.
> I am with you.

She closed her eyes and tried to remember exactly what he looked like but couldn't. Somehow her two would-be defilers had been mixed inextricably in her reverie. As she lay in bed at night, her fists up her labia minora, all she could focus on was a blur of almost-rapists who had almost saved her day but not quite.

She waited for the light to change and three Alpha Sigmas cut right in front of her without even looking up. She parted her lips a little, fluffed her hair, and breathed heavily through her nostrils, making them open and close passionately, like a guppy breathing out of water. Then she ran her tongue over her mouth to make it moist and gummy, but they didn't even wait for the light. They knew, just like they'd known in high school, that while they were playing with themselves to The Amboy Dukes, she had a subscription to *Seventeen*.

"Nice girls do," she called after them, but there were so many sluts, who needed her? Why was it all she'd ever found was a forestry senior who was saving his pure untouched body for his future wife, a blond twin with rheumatic heart fever who had strict orders from his doctor, and the two not-quite-almost rapists from the panty raid?

She decided to cut through the park. Surely, in a park, at dusk, a girl took her virginity in her hands. "Oh Lord," she moaned, "I'm practically a registered voter —and what do I have to show for it? I'm not even nicked, let alone damaged beyond repair. . . ."

It was late and the park was almost empty. There was only one little kid left in the sandbox. He wore corduroy overalls and a blue-and-red-striped T-shirt. He was pouring sand from one orange juice container to another and looked up blankly as she passed.

"Hi," she said, but he quickly put his head back to his business again. Then, right after she passed, but while she was still in earshot, he said: "Titty-sucking, mother-fucking, no-headed nothing," which meant, she was positive, she was a walking roadsign. It also meant his mother rushed over with a Wash'n'dry to clean his mouth out, and come between them. "You whore . . ." she cried.

I should be so lucky, Amy thought, slumping into a distant bench, suddenly terrified if she played with herself one more time, something important might work loose, maybe even get stuck up there where even a gynecologist wouldn't be able to find it.

> You are mine, I am yours.
> Soon. Sooner than you think.

said the third note this week.

"How many times do I have to tell you to let a boy do it," her mother threatened, but what was she supposed to do? Run an ad in the *Penny Saver*? and besides, somehow she didn't think her mother meant the kind of boy who carried sticks.

> I know where you're going.
> I know where you've been. . . .

Four men as old as her father walked by lusting after her. She knew it, the way they nudged each other and each imagined to themselves what a nice girl like that was doing walking alone at dusk through a park. She could even see their flies at full tilt, and how they had to limp with the weight.

The little boy's mother took him out of the sandbox and carried him home screaming under her armpit. Then the only other person in the whole park was a little old man at the other end who held his wrinkled raisin head up into the leaves of the aspens, and called into the trees. The sounds he made were sucked up into the flickering of the leaves and the rest of the dying day. And still he called again and again, this yesterday vendor: "I cash memories. . . ."

He made a circle and called again: "Here, Luche. Here Luche *mía*," walking down one end of the park and up another, but Amy didn't want to know what he'd lost.

She was suddenly aware that she didn't want to know for a lot of different reasons and that one of them was that then she'd never be able to leave. That she'd have to join him and spend the rest of her life, too, with her head up in the park poplars. Which, she supposed, did make her a nice girl. A nice girl who once lost a Shirley Temple doll on a bus and still mourned for her.

"*Ven acá, Luche mía*," he called. "Come to papa."

Please, don't come any closer, she said into her lap. Losses were permanent scars, I don't want to know about yours. She still remembered that Shirley Temple had had rubber curlers and two six-guns packed in real leather holsters, so no wonder it was hard to get laid, even in a panty raid.

"*Ven acá!*" Closer and closer. "Here Luche," the little man, searching hopelessly, desperately, and in his hand an empty bird cage. So she wouldn't look, not up into the trees where his lifelong companion had flown never to sing again. To be eaten by a peregrine falcon. To be asphyxiated by a diesel truck. To what? She looked away from the little man, who probably had a little mother at home who made him tortillas in the morning and buñuelos at night. And empanadas, empanaditas, gorditas compuestas, and parakeet stew.

Two kids about ten wheeled their bikes across the square right in front of her, and the little old raisin man came up and asked them if they'd seen a burd.

Sure they seen a burd, they said. They'd seen alotta burds, and rode off thumbing their hineys, leaving only her.

Her, he came towards, wanting. With the shiny wet tears down his walnut cheeks. But before he had a chance, before he headed her down another *Seventeen* alley, she grabbed her pocketbook with the notes and got the hell out of there.

"The hell with your billet-doux," she screamed into the trees. "It's now or never!" She turned and lifting her skirts over her head, leapfrogged over the seesaws and the water fountains. "Come and get it," she hollered, and she was sure she saw his orange reindeer over there somewhere, but all she came away with was the sound of his laughing.

Don't worry, it sounded like, the laughing. . . . Don't worry, I will!

· 23 ·

and explained how Mort was closing in on him with the
Trinidad Lucero Defense Fund, Billy said the only way
to shut up a guy like Mort was to ambush him on his
own turf. Swallow him. Bury him in the bowels of the
earth. When Trini hung up he stunk from his own
sweat. He slumped to his knees and faced the blue bathtub Cremencio Ortega had set into the corner of the
room and left for Trini as a gesture of hope. Cremencio
had had to take, though it pained him, the virgin, who
had previously rested in the tub shrine, because his
mother had made him promise before she died that he
would keep her with him always, but Trini said to him-

self that her spirit lingered on, and it might turn out to be better than nothing.

"Oh, Lord," Trini intoned, "I don't want no trouble. I'm a good Catholic boy, who has prayed on his knees for as long as I can remember." But the wheels of fortune had already been set in motion, and all because of Ashley's little bottle of bogus promises.

Trini spent a long time on the phone with Billy, begging him to find another way, but before he hung up Billy had said take it or leave it, and what choice did Trini have?

Not that Trini was the only one in trouble. The President of the University, President Priestly, had seen to it to destroy Lester Newbauer as well, though it was only a coincidence that Lester's letter canceling his scholarship was postmarked the same day that Trini got through to Billy Dawson, who was almost never home.

It seemed that Lester's putting up the poster in the library had been enough to disqualify him for any further university aid. For as President Priestly wrote, as of the above date, Lester Newbauer had forfeited all rights to any and all scholarships, fellowships, or assistantships said university had, or might some day have to offer. Tacking up the poster to SAVE LUCERO in the library had constituted soliciting for political purposes on university property, and so his free ride had, after fourteen years, come to a dead stop, and high time, too.

The worst of it was that Ron Harkness, psychological

counselor, could find nothing better than, "I told you so," with which to assuage his bereft lover. He couldn't even resist shaking his finger, which hurt worse than Lester's burping stomach that, ever since the mail came, hurt more up around his heart than down near the duodenum, meaning something Lester could no longer remember.

· 24 ·

"DON'T TELL ME YOU DIDN'T, Rhile saw you."

"What do you mean *saw*, and keep your voice down."

"Is that all you have to worry about? I tell you your own son saw you and all you can say is keep your voice down?" He slammed a clenched fist into his palm.

"I go off to work thinking my wife lies convalescing and find out from my own son you're fornicating your head off with some neighbor kid. Fornicating in plain view of my son. *My son!*" he repeated, hanging his head. "Is that what a man should come home to after a hard day's work?"

"For heaven's sake, Mort."

"Don't for heaven's sake *me*," he said. "One unborn

seedling within and a stripling watching their mother fucking like an alley cat! I suppose . . ."

"You don't have to swear."

"I'm sorry. I suppose you thought I wouldn't find out. Well! You had another think coming, I can tell you. You just didn't count on how close I am to that boy, that's what you didn't count on."

And then, again he remembered and forgot Lucero and having to call him. And what was he to do, explain how he had the boy crouched behind his mother's dresser and how he'd seen everything? Well, why not— he was sure Lucero would understand the predicament he was in and how he just couldn't come right away, or get the Defense Fund going. Especially after he'd given the full particulars. About her faithlessness and everything. He thought maybe he'd even call that nice Lester Newbauer and tell him, too. Oh, he thought, it was a blessing, to have good friends in a time of crisis!

"How could you?" he said. She poured him another cup of alfalfa tea and told him to drink it, it was good for him.

She was telling *him*, the nymphomaniac? He sighed again.

"What?"

"When I slave all day to give you a decent roof over your head and the head of your son!"

"Oh!"

She took another cup herself.

"You'll wake the boy," she said, "do you want some honey in it? You're making a hill of beans into a mole-hill." She shifted her weight, as it was really getting hard to sit in one position. Mort got up to pace so she relaxed. This was not the first time he'd paced. She looked at the cracks in the ceiling and decided that some looked like antelopes. If only he'd bring it all to a head; he took so long about everything. . . .

But Mort had begun carefully to peel the casing from a slice of wurst. Deftly scraping so as to get every bit of meat. Then he wiped the knife meticulously over and over, poking up inside the blade connection with the napkin wrapped around his fingernail. Every so often he'd lower hurt eyes on her, but didn't say anything. He was concentrating. If only she could see the kind of pain she brought him, and once again he thought how nothing, not even freedom, no, not any cause, could cut as deeply as the meandering of true love. . . .

Ashley fixed the barrette in her hair.

But he felt guilty anyway . . . shirking Trinidad Lucero now that he needed him. Oh, when would she ever learn there was a time and place for everything. . . .

"But . . ." He let out a world-weary sigh, threw his hands into the air, and then let them fall heavily around his knees.

Ashley got ready.

"O.K.," he said, "you were depressed. I can understand that. What woman wouldn't be depressed to almost lose a child. A child of her loins!" His eyes watered. He leaned forward to rub her belly for luck. "Besides," he murmured, "who could blame you, considering your background." (Considering your mother's practically a whore, considering I picked you up out of the gutter out of the goodness of my heart, considering . . .) And Rhile quietly eased his door open and sat in the night shadows listening. "Not I. No, it just isn't my personality to condemn a woman and you know it. Perhaps," and he looked deep into her eyes, "perhaps you even banked on that, that I would accept, and say nothing. Well?"

"Well, nothing."

"Well, God knows, he's not the first. . . ."

"Oh, get on with it, Mort."

"I should get on with it, you say, well, as my wife you might have considered, oh, never mind," he said as she cracked a couple of sunflower seeds.

"I suppose you're right."

"What?"

"It probably is half my fault."

She spread the thick basswood honey on some bread.

"After all," he said. "No man is an island."

Hurry up, she whispered to herself. Get it over with . . .

"I can see I'm boring you." And he paused, but as she refused to get in on it, he went on. "All right. All right, I've decided, that is, if you're still interested . . ."

"Yes, Mort," she said. "I'm still interested." And since when did she have to be interested? . . . Wasn't it enough she had to sit there and listen?

"Now, you may be surprised by my generosity and don't interrupt. I have decided that your lover, this Mendola boy, can move in with us."

"Naturally," she said. She shook her head languidly and his words flew through her mind like the barn swallows she had once.

"Of course, I'll continue to support the family as I've always done. For to me, the family, the root of society, will always be . . . has always been, the most important consideration. Even if emotionally we go our separate ways," he said, and she knew he'd say it.

He said, "Genero—his name is Genero, isn't it?—can move his things right into the bedroom and I'll fix myself a couch in the living room. Ashley? Are you listening, Ashley?"

"Uh huh," she said. By this time she had decided that the cracks in the ceiling looked more like sheared sheep.

Then he told her how they could knock out a wall and add another room. She had been waiting all night for this part, about knocking out the wall. He asked her if she thought Genero would like that. And he also knew that the father's name was Amarante, the mother's, Carmen. That they had four sons, Genero, Manuel, Leandro, and Perfecto, who lived over in Rankin and kept goats.

"I could set up my lab in the larger of the two rooms, maybe your Genero would take an interest. . . . For are we not as polyseeds in a single sunflower? And is not man aught but a time-binder?"

What, the little boy wondered, what is man?

"Ah yes," Mort said. "For man is not on this world in his nakedness. . . . And does not the son need the father? One another," he said. "We need. You and I. Our progeny and us. Aah," he touched her belly and she began to unbutton her blouse. Then she pulled down the straps of her slip as the little boy crawled down the hall on his tummy as slow and quiet as Yigal Allon.

His mother's belly was very big as it slithered out of her skirt, and his daddy's hands had liver spots all over them because how many times had she told him to take Vitamin E and he wouldn't? Then he got up on top of her the way the boy did who gave him a pocketful of pinion nuts. Why did they do that? That's what he couldn't figure out, and finally the light went off and all he could see was a big black shadow that looked like an elephant climbing out of an ostrich shell.

· 25 ·

MARTIN W. SAMUELS HAD
already found Mr. Keene, the famous tracer, through
the out-of-print Yellow Pages in the archives of the
main library, and now there was nothing to do but wait.

He'd dug out a tassle from the flowered chintz chaise
his wife used to have in the bedroom and sent it along
as a sample of his son's spit, along with three pairs of
the kid's unwashed diapers, but those he'd had to take
out of the gold frames they'd been kept in since the
time Jack was born. It hurt to give up relics of such
sentiment, but if ever the little snot-nosed shitass was to
be found, he would have to be ruthless with his tender
sensibilities . . . absolutely ruthless.

· 26 ·

AS FAR AS INTRIGUE WAS concerned, Billy Dawson would rather pick his nose, but by now the kike was an obsession. He'd felt so much better after their last encounter that he drove from Lester's directly to spic town and almost got it up three times in a row. Just about up and just about in, clean as Hemingway, that's how good it felt. So, when the greaser called him, he was ready, all right. Sure, he said, sure he'd get the yid off the greaser's neck for him, but he insisted on catching him by surprise.

"You see, this petition, if he goes out and raises money . . . it will create the wrong impression," the greaser said on the phone. "You see," but Billy didn't see shit. All he saw were Mort Dralon's eyes and the chance for him to once again become the biggest stud on campus.

Doris Day sang *"Que Será Será"* on Billy's Buick radio as he drove in and out of the passing lanes at seventy and sometimes seventy-five, but Trini wasn't listening. Now Trini had troubles about and beyond Mort Dralon. The other morning in the mail he'd received a letter with an El Paso postmark and for two days it had sat unopened on the table in the hallway next to all the other drop dead letters he'd been receiving, ten, twenty at a time. But, when finally he did take a knife to it, it turned out to be a death certificate with his own name on it and written in Spanish and English. It was signed by his father, the attending physician, Dr. Ysofio Lucero-Casadas, and witnessed by his two brothers, Manny and Solvio. He didn't care how fast Billy drove.

The letter started him shivering, *"Aye,* Papa. You *no comprende,* es Stravinsky, not your own Trini, who is the Russian. *America,* Charles Ives's *America,* is to do with diminished sevenths, papa, not the Monroe Doctrine. . . ." And what could he do more? Write home and remind them who it was who single-handedly gave it to Socrates?

Up ahead was a sign: EATS. Beyond was darkness.

"What's that you do with your fingers?" Billy asked him, at the sound of Trini's swollen knuckles cracking apart and cracking together. He sat on his hands. His lips quivered, but it was dark in the car. They began

· 155 ·

to slow down, and after Billy flew by the little greasy spoon, they backed up and parked. From the other direction, the sign read: STAE. It reminded Billy of home. Of Lubbock and Mama and eating till you were so full you weren't hungry again till you walked out the door. Crap, Billy said, home was where the ass was. He pushed through the door with the broken screen; a couple of pimpled cowboys sat at the counter. Billy walked by them looking for a fight.

> Cold taters ne'er did taste good . . .
> Chicken on the plate.

The jukebox was too loud.

> My mother used to say to me, Jim,
> Take an old cold tater and wait.

When they kept on drinking their Cokes, he sat at a table that had a top made from the linoleum left over from the bathroom floor. He knew without looking that the bathroom hook on the door wouldn't work. They never did. The fluorescent tube over the fry range kept blinking on and off, and if it wasn't Lubbock, it was what Lubbock had come to be in his nightmares.

"Yeah?" she said, the waitress in a white stained uniform you could see though to the black slip and pink bra underneath. Billy would have liked to give it to her, not down there, but right between the eyes, the Woolworth slob. He hated her type, with her head all done up like cotton candy.

The jukebox blared on:

> Tater and waaaaiiit
> Tater and waaaaaaaiiiiiiiiit
> Tater and waaaaaaaaaaaaaaaaaiiiiiiiiiiiit!!

He felt a hot shudder travel down his spine and then ordered liver and onions. Trini, for his part, thought she was beautiful, with her white Anglo skin and her yellow Anglo hair. He said "please" two times when he ordered. "Could I please have a cup of tea, please?" which really pissed Billy. Then he called her "Miss."

Billy watched her swing along over to the counter, waving her ass, and she reminded him of Smilin' Jack's fat sidekick, whatsisname. The one with the buttons that kept popping off. There was a line of pink grease around her face that stopped at her chin, and she made him puke. The jukebox finally came to a frantic stop. All you could hear was the hum of the fluorescent tubing over the fry range. Then, for no reason, he remembered Lester Newbauer's ass again. The feel of it all over his cock, the way it pressed in and held him. Fuck you, Newbauer, everybody *doesn't* do it at least once. I bet this lily-livered shitmouse greaser next to me never even picks his navel. But again he felt Lester's cheeks closing him in, pillowing him to the devil's eternity.

Why liver and onions? Trini thought, when Billy went to the can. He only hoped he could keep down the tea, get it over with, get going. He also wished his life had started and stopped on the podium on the stage of the Alameda High School. He was afraid he was going to Frijolito, New Mexico, en route to the gas chamber. He was afraid that Billy Dawson couldn't get rid of Mort a second time. He was afraid the tea would stir up some peristaltic action he couldn't control.

Billy came back and drew one leg over the back of the chair when he sat down. Then his liver came. The waitress went back for the onions and the home-fried potatoes and the ketchup. Trini cracked his knuckles till they ached. Billy looked at him with tiny slit eyes and said, "Quit it," and just then the front door opened and in walked a kid not more than nineteen, wearing a white shirt open at the neck and a pair of khaki chinos.

"O.K., lady," the kid said, "this is a stickup."

She didn't seem to hear him, so he said it again. But Billy heard him the first time. Right away he stopped chewing and raised his head. The kid was carrying a gun which he had pointed straight at the waitress, who now had her head cocked to one side like a broken kewpie doll. No, it wasn't that she wasn't listening. It was more like she was listening to somebody on television.

"Now, don't get riled," the kid said. "Just open the till and that'll be that."

Trini heard Billy say, "Holy shit," and felt a sudden fear.

"That's some big mother," Billy said, "would you look at that. How come you need a goddamn .32 for a lousy six-buck job?" he asked the kid.

"No," Trini whispered and pulled on his knuckles.

The kid didn't say anything. He just kept his eye on the salt lady and told her again, "Look, lady, just empty the cash from the till! I ain't gonna hurt you."

But by this time Billy was Humphrey Bogart in *The Petrified Forest*. On his feet, with shoulder pads. Only it was Ashley Wilkes who had the gun. And Bette Davis over there in the corner next to the cornflakes, with lumpy mascara tears halfway down her thick pastel cheeks.

"Are you crazy?" Trini whispered, but Billy only laughed. "Your fucking A," he said. How often did a guy get a chance to stand up to a .32 in Humphrey Bogart's white and tan spectators?

"Don't," Trini begged him.

"Screw off."

"The boy's got a gun. A *gun*, how do you know it's not loaded? Not now," he whimpered, "when we're so close!"

But Humphrey shrugged off the Jew who could sing for his ambush. Loaded was what everything was about.

"Let's go," Trini whispered. But Billy said to the kid, "Hey there, fellah." And he kind of ambled nearer. "Why don't you put down the old heater there, boy?" making Trini sink down behind the table onto his knees.

Trini crawled over to Billy's pants leg and tugged at the edge of the cuff.

"Quit it, spic." Billy gave his leg a quick shake, knocking off Trini's swollen knuckles onto the linoleum.

"Why don't we have us a cup of java?"

The kid wheeled around and pointed the big gun at Billy.

"Take it easy," Billy said, raising his palm. "Just take it nice and easy, boy."

"And don't call me *boy*."

"We're going to be late." Trini talked right into a line of stitching around the bottom of Billy's jeans. "How are we going to find this Dralon's house in the dark?"

Billy took another step. And if any one of those twats he hadn't been able to touch with a ten-inch cock could see him now, they'd know what he's made of. And so would Lester Newbauer. Would the thought of a girl's wootsie come to Lester Newbauer at a time like this?

"Be a good kid," he heard himself say, "and give us the gat."

He took another step towards him. And then Trini got up on his feet and said in a very loud voice: "This is silly!"

"Mind your own goddamn business," Billy said to him.

"How can you think of cops and robbers at a time like this?"

"Screw off, just screw the fuck off," and a third time he turned back to the kid and asked for the gun.

"I'm warning you," the kid said again, "stay where you are. I'll use it," but Billy didn't stay where he was. He took another step toward him and Trini sank back down in the chair. "*Que será será*," he said to himself, and moved Billy's liver and onions closer to him—at the same time pouring out a lot of ketchup.

"I'm telling you," the kid screamed again and the knuckles on his gun hand tensed red and white. Nothing was going the way it was supposed to. The girl was supposed to be alone like she always was at closing in the middle of the week. How come she wasn't? How come? and he waved the .32 back and forth between the cash register and Billy Dawson.

"Open the till, damnit. Goddamnit, lady, open the till!" Then he swung towards Billy again and shouted, "O.K., you're so smart, you tell her. You tell her to open up."

But Billy just said, real calm-like, "It's all over kid." He was swaggering a little and Trini Lucero was eating so fast he was swallowing the rubbery skin around the liver right down with the slippery onions. And right then Billy felt an unfamiliar, reedy, *ping* sensation, accompanied by a high, fast sound/scratch, in the middle of his guts. "It's all over kid," he said, words from the silver screen, where holes dripped the same ketchup that was all over Trini Lucero's mouth.

Then the kid swerved towards the register with the jolt of the shot and Trini picked up what was left of the liver and began chewing on it like corn on the cob.

"No," the kid muttered. The broad was supposed to have opened up right off and he was supposed to have grabbed the dough and that was supposed to be that. "Open up, damn you. . . ." He was crying. But the fellow who wasn't supposed to be there kept right on coming, which got him so mad he shot him again.

"You shouldn't of done that," Billy said. And he called him "fellah" again. He grabbed for the second pinngg-prick in his belly but moved right ahead anyway. Why?

Why did he walk?

He was shot in the belly and he knew it. Any moron could see he was shot in the belly, so why was he still walking? You didn't see the filthy slut over there walking, hell no, she was backed up against the cereals like one more Grape-Nuts Flakes, or the fat-assed greaser either, down his shiny knees saying a goddamn rosary with a goddamn knotted handkerchief . . . you didn't see him walking ahead, either, with a bellyful of bullets.

"You know you're gonna give it to me," he said. And he had his hand out for it. Again, why? Why the fuck did he want it?

Nobody even there to even notice.

While the kid got more and more frantic, still walking towards him. And him bleeding, for godsakes, right through his fingers and down his pants.

"I hate you," the kid screamed. "I hate you," and he shot him again and then ran through the front door shaking like all get out.

This time the bullet tore through Billy's shoulder and hit the wall next to the doughnuts. And this time it hurt. And the other little holes too. All of a sudden Billy didn't know which hurt worse. Exit Humphrey Bogart. With the sound of the slammed door, hurt was all there was. The pain tore right through him. Dear God almighty!!! He was really *shot*! Smart Billy from Lubbock . . . ? Shot in the gut? What for? I did it, he told himself, I let myself get shot, but what the fucking hell for? Why, I wonder, did I let myself get shot? Why? And then holding a sopping stomach, he lurched forward onto the floor and fell into a bleeding heap.

"Holy Mary, Mother of God," whispered Trini Lucero, "I knew it. Now we'll never stop the Trinidad Lucero Defense Committee."

Billy moaned. He had passed out. Trini got up and went over to him. His blood was trickling onto the floor. He watched it mush up with the dirt and run through the tire marks of somebody's Mexican sandals. And then the waitress came to life. She began shrieking and crying so that the rouge on her cheeks turned to paste.

"Stop it!" Billy screamed through his coma, but his voice never made it to the surface. "Stop it, I can't stand the noise. I can't stand it, I tell you, please stop it." But nobody heard him. He had passed out. How were they to know he couldn't stand the noise? And the next minute he wasn't passed out. "Please," he begged, "make her stop, I'm dying." But it wasn't any better. He was up but his voice still wasn't.

He inched a trembling hand over towards the greaser's bended knee and whispered, "What the fucking hell's the matter with you, can't you recognize death when it spits in your eye?" But before Trini got close enough to hear, he'd passed out again. Out then in. Out and then in again.

The next time he came to, the spic was saying, "I'll

call the police." The pussy was still screaming. This time it was Billy's turn to catch Trini by the trouser cuff.

"Not the police, you idiot, hell," he said, "get me to a doctor before I die all over this goddamn floor."

"Not the police, you idiot," Trini said like a parrot. What he should do was he should call a doctor. But how could he call a doctor? To call a doctor he had to have a dime, but he didn't have a dime. So he looked through all his pockets and said, "Who's got a dime?"

"Do you have a dime?" he said to the waitress. "Two dimes and a nickel for a quarter, maybe?" And the waitress just stood there shaking her head while Billy passed out twice more and came to again.

He isn't, Billy told himself between one coma and the next, this dumb fucking cocksucker isn't looking through all his pockets for a dime while I bleed to death? Dying, for crissakes, right in front of him, this isn't the way old B.D. gets his, it just isn't happening.

"Never mind the dime. My car," he whispered through the pain. But Trini didn't hear him, so he raised his head off the floor and tried again.

"Take my car, you moron. My car," and passed out.

His car. You're to take his car. Sure, you're to take his car and take him to a doctor because he's been shot three times. But if he's the one shot three times, how come it says Trinidad Lucero on the death certificate signed by your father in Spanish and English?

· 27 ·

TRINI LEFT BILLY AT HOLY
Innocents' Hospital, strapped to a metal operating table
with a great glaring light burning into his eyeballs. He
had come to long enough to call the nun who was
swabbing his arm a dumb, shit-assed motherfucker.

Then Trini took a room at the Lorraine Hotel,
afraid if he went home Mort Dralon would find him.
He ended up sleeping for twelve hours and had to pay
for two nights because he passed the checkout time.
But Mort, of course, never showed. Because Mort was
busy investigating *why* Ashley had almost lost his seed.
And not only why, but how!

He put the bottle of medicine Ashley had gotten
from the doctor in Gallup in the middle of the table

so she could see he knew. But, after moving it once next to the bottle of soy granules and then between the sautéd brains and the millet, he could see that she had made up her mind not to see no matter where he put it. So he said, "I did a little investigating."

"That's nice," she said and took a Vitamin A.

"Don't you want to know what?"

"Sure." Then she took a Vitamin E.

"I'll bet," he said as he watched her mix a little dolomite with the cottage cheese.

"You know darn well what I investigated. Only, you don't know what I found out, that's what you don't know," pushing the incriminating bottle right over in front of her plate, while Trini Lucero stayed away from his apartment three days in a row just in case.

"What did you find out?" Ashley asked him, blaming herself because of the bad planning. Better timing, she figured, would have forestalled this little episode altogether.

"This time it's serious," he said.

She told Rhile to drink his milk.

"I mean it, Lee."

"Should I cut you an apple, Rhile? Do you want a nice fresh apple? I wonder if they spray these apples. Mort? Do you think they sp——"

"I said it's serious."

"Well, spraying apples is . . ."

"I don't think you get the full significance of what you've done. That child is half mine. My seed is in that child."

"Not in front of the child."

"What do you mean, not in front of the child! Don't you think the child ought to know what kind of mother he has?"

"Yes, Mommy, don't you think I should?"

"Drink your milk, Rhile."

"Daddy?"

"Your mother's right, drink your milk, Rhile. What you've done is you've tried to murder my child," he said, suddenly turning away from Rhile and bringing his face very close to Ashley's.

"What child? Did Mommy try to murder me, Daddy?"

"No, Mommy didn't try to murder you. Finish your milk and go out and play."

"What is the matter with you, Mort?"

"Me? The matter with me? I leave you alone and . . . Well, let me tell you, a little private-eye work pays off."

"What's a private eye?"

"And I know where you got the stuff."

"What stuff?"

"Go out and play."

"But I didn't finish my milk."

"And you didn't hide it too well, either."

"Hide? I didn't hide anything."

"She did, she did, I saw her. What? What did she hide?"

"Nothing, Rhile, finish your milk. Oh? Then why was it down behind the dresser?"

"And what does a bottle behind the dresser prove?" (A little bogus bottle that promised free passage and delivered only a bellyache.) She got up to boil some more water for tea.

"The date," he said. "Read it." He grabbed the bottle and shoved it up to her nose.

"You're going to be late."

"What time's it?"

"Ten of."

"I tell you, read the date on that label. . . . Never mind, I'll read it myself. It was Friday the seventeenth, which makes you a fifth column in this family."

"What's a fifth column?"

"*Our* family, Ashley Dralon. Deny you went behind my back to destroy the fruit of my loins. . . . My seed! That you brought another man to my bed . . ."

"I saw him."

"What, who did you see, Rhiley Piley?"

"The man Mommy brought to her bed."

"Of course you saw him. . . . See? See, your own son saw him. Now deny you have plotted against the sanctity of this precious trilogy! The sanctuary of our very family! You deny it?"

"I did, Mommy. I did too saw him."

"And this bottle. Tell me this isn't foul brew, sneaked out and paid for behind my back, with the profits of the sweat of my brow. . . ."

"For heaven's sake, Mort, quit it."

But Morton Milton Dralon had no intention of quitting anything. She should have thought about quitting before she messed with him. For, as he wagged a finger in the air, that much she should, after all this time, know. . . . When Mort put his shoulder to the wheel that's where it stayed. Except in cases of extreme emergency, like for instance his commitment to the Trinidad Lucero Defense Committee, but what was he to do? As history was his judge. With such a helpmeet at his side. . . . Did he have any other choice?

"Abortion is a serious offense," he said. "Plotting to destroy a man's very seed! And especially, didn't I offer him a home in my home? A place on your pillow?"

"Genero had nothing to do with it."

"Aha!" he cried, "so you admit it."

"I have to make."

"You admit deliberate and cold-blooded murder aforethought. . . ."

"Daddy . . ."

"What?"

"I have to make, Daddy."

"Well? Do you? Make, go make," he said. "And was I unreasonable? Did I deserve such repayment after I even offered to put the very food in your lover's mouth?"

"What's a lover?"

"Or weren't the pleasures of my bed enough for him?"

"I told you, he had nothing to do with it, and you're too late."

"She told you, he had nothing to do . . ."

"I thought you had to make."

"Need anything from the store?"

"Duz," she said. He stopped to pick up the boy's water pistol.

"Mommy?"

"What?"

"I made in my pants."

"Why didn't you go make?"

"How could the boy make at a time like this? . . . a time of such moral indecision . . . with such sociological ramifi——"

"You're going to be late for school."

"What else?"

"Apples maybe. Two pounds, and I don't know what else, I can't seem to find the list. What time will you be home?"

"Why?"

"Oh, for godsakes, Mort, no special reason."

"Oh," he said, "I thought. . . ."

"I know what you thought, but I told you, it's over," and of that she was sure. Not only did the doctor in Gallup let her down, but what lover would put up with an outraged husband who not only didn't try and kill him, but instead invited him to become an integral factor in the, as Mort called it, intimate family structure? If Ashley wasn't sure of another thing, she was sure of that. It was good and over with Genero Mendola all right. . . .

So Mort put the water pistol down on the table, wrote down Duz and apples, and got to his first afternoon class just in time for Hector Velásquez to finish the horns on his portrait of the teacher, which was quite good, especially around the deep furrows over the glassed-in eyes.

· 28 ·

STRAPPED INTO A HOSPITAL
bed, Billy Dawson had very little to do besides relive
past glories. He refought his bulls, *mano-a-mano, a las
quatro de la tarde, punto,* won old bets over and over
and strangled his mother's worn-out old suitors. Then,
four nights in a row, he lived again the crash of the big
navy transport. He saw the seven cadets splinter in the
sky. He saw the second seven cadets shit in their pants
and he saw himself go on up in his single-seater, as if
nothing had ever splashed the air with blood.

"That's me," he murmured to the nurse with the hair
on her upper lip, when she wandered in and out with
her hypos. "See me, up there in the stratosphere, being
mighty. See me take them all through their paces, Navy

Cadet Billy Dawson. Admire me, touch me, ain't I grand?"

Control Tower to CX 4 told him to advance the throttle, that first totally free moment in the clouds. Control also told him to lean the mixture. But nobody could tell Billy Dawson to feel the rise of the world or his power over it. About the sudden knowledge that there was never anything between you and the old sonofabitch, ever. Fuck you, Lubbock, he whistled through his teeth. The same pile of kitties under his mother's bed. The same smell of armpit in the bacon grease. Billy Dawson had the world by the neck, what did he need Lubbock for?

In high school they used to call his mother a whore, but she wasn't. Really, she was just a sap. She wasn't smart enough to be a whore. He floated around on the empty sky and could see her open another can of Franco-American. He dipped his wings in and out of the mashed potato clouds and Old Man Death could pick his nose till it bled. Did that sound like somebody Lester Newbauer could pluke up the ass? He asked him. Then he murmured, "Help," through his delirium and the nun came in and snickered over him.

He flew around twenty minutes before his stainless-steel, shock-resistant, water-repellent, antimagnetic chronometer told him it was three o'clock. He remembered because that was three minutes before the engine went out. He heard it. Humming at three, dead three minutes later, and out the window, he was sure he saw the silhouette of the big transport again. He felt the impact and the heat of the burning bodies. But not me, he whispered . . . and I don't care if the engine's deader than the black ace. It's O.K. for the slobs, let them call home to Control. Let them pee in their pants. The echoless nothing means seven, come eleven to me. Boxcars, five spades, and a steady pulse.

O.K., I'll call, but just for show. This could turn into my exit visa. I'll call and go on record. But fear all over Billy Dawson's forehead like acne? Fuck off.

He called. He riched the mixture. He turned on the booster pump. He threw open the throttle and he told them the gauges said nothing.

"Maintain flying speed," they said, and the altimeter dove down faster than a ten-pound test, stuck down the craw of a Hemingway marlin.

"Do you see anything?" they asked him, their voices all choked up. Two crashes in two days meant their asses in a sling, but not Billy's. Death just didn't turn him on.

"Twenty-one thousand," he said. "Altimeter falling fast."

"Switch the gas tanks," they said, and "prime the engine." But what Billy was talking about was the game. What did Control know about hitchhiking through childhood on the back end of flammable oil trucks?

It didn't matter if Billy didn't see anything when they said, "Look." It wasn't over yet, not by a dead-eye. It'd be there, the emergency landing field. That's what winning was all about.

"Hang on," they told him. "Hang on, fellah, we're sending a search plane," and Billy saw Myrna Loy, back at the hangar, wringing transparent hands and snuffling.

"Fifteen hundred, but maintaining speed. Where's the goddamn field? Where is it?" He moaned for their benefit. "Where is it?" so it would look good when later he pleaded inability to cope. He held one hand over his mouth to keep from laughing and then decided it was a good time to start losing contact. He thumped the earphones a few times and screamed into the mike.

Are you digging this, Lester Newbauer, you fag freak? Are you getting the picture? See who you're dealing with? And then, for a minute, he did feel. Not fear. Not the slow rush of anguish through his bowels, but something like it. The fast realization that he should have. That it was odd, his feeling nothing, when, at that very second, up it came, the earth, fast into his face and how could he be so sure?

"Can you hear us, CX 4? . . . Come in, can you hear us?"

Again he switched the radio on and off and let them get a few words about wanting to bail out at a thousand feet. About the orchards up ahead mined with bayonets. Then out again. He sat back and knew he was O.K. because not even a part of his life passed in front of his eyes. Not even the sounds of mother-fucking, back in Lubbock. Or the Smilin' Jack comics, page by page, while he waited out on the back porch for whoever it was to zip up and move out smartly.

"They've spotted you," Control said, "CX 4, hang on. They're coming. They've spotted you."

And then he spotted his field. Right where it should have been, perfect to the detail of a road wriggling through a distant hill like a grass snake after a lightning bug.

"Don't despair, use your head, save your hair." All of a sudden he panicked. He remembered his mother's dusty brown Philco with the missing volume knob. Phil Harris and Alice Faye. The Fitch Bandwagon, was that part of his life? Wasn't the emergency landing field his royal flush after all?

"Ninety-six longitude," they were telling him. "Do you read me, CX 4? Ninety-six longitude . . ." but from then on it was like taking bacon and eggs from W. C. Fields. It was his field, all right, a mile wide and thick with alfalfa. No dramatic flames of iridescent green. No brass band obbligato, and pretty soon he passed under their line of sight, and bye bye Alice Faye. . . .

He gave the old Boy Scout smile to the search plane and then lowered his nose just right. Enough to land her but not enough to drop like a goddamn rock. In twenty minutes the crash truck was there with the blanket and the brandy and he thought back to the slobs with fear over their foreheads with a little envy. It mightn't be so bad, to feel indecision, to know what it was to grab hard to one reality, fearful of having to switch it mid-stream for another.

"Some harrowing experience, buddy," the guy in the flight jacket said, offering him his hand, but Billy was ready for him. He kicked him hard in the groin and had to force himself to holler as he stomp-jumped the other two, so it would look good for the head shrinkers. So that they'd have no choice but put down on their Section Eight discharge that he'd never be able to go up again without cracking right down the middle, probably due to some tragic flaw in his childhood.

· 29 ·

"WELL, I DON'T KNOW," SHE said coyly when he finally jumped out from between two parked cars into the light. He wore the same orange ski sweater, argyle socks, a St. Christopher medal around his neck, and an open fly, so Amy never even noticed the scabs all over his arms.

She twirled the ends of her hair around her fingers and could feel the inside of her virginity pursing its lips together.

"Don't give me 'you don't know.' You know."

"But it's so sudden." She smiled and tried to pretend they weren't standing on Coal and Hermosilla, at three o'clock in the morning, in front of a two-family house with a sign in the front yard that said UPHOLSTERY.

"It's now or never, sister," he said to her, and poked two fingers further up her than she'd thought possible.

This is it, she told herself. She wrapped her legs around his hand and pushed it in further. This is really, after all this time, the big it. I am practically home.

"Do it now," Amy moaned into his ear, but he only hissed at her.

"What do you think we're getting married for? To do it now I don't need to invest in a Wassermann test."

And so it was that Amy Collins became officially engaged.

"Who the hell is Jack Samuels?" her father, the Legislative Guild Representative, asked once or twice in a lucid moment, but before it became necessary for Amy to think of something to tell him, the phone would ring and her father would automatically go and hide under the studio couch. Trini Lucero called moment by moment, but the Legislative Guild Representative had no intention of compromising himself by answering. Why only yesterday he'd read in the *Herald* that Nikolai Lobachevski had formulated a concept of non-Euclidean geometry. It was a complete accident, and he'd had no intention of reading it. It had been slipped in between two other articles, one on Daylight Savings Time and the other advertising a sale of Castro Convertibles. He'd immediately covered the paper with his hand, even though it was in his own kitchen. Then he'd made a very large point of shaking his head back and forth and saying, "Tsk, tsk, the nerve of him. You had to watch them every minute, those Russkies." Not answering the telephone was just one of the ways Dave Collins saw of stopping the threat of encroaching Communism.

"That was in eighteen twenty-five, Daddy," his daughter crooned to him as he lay on his belly under the couch, "the Lobachevski formula, we studied that in . . ."

"You, too?" he moaned. "Has it spread as far as my own home already?"

But Amy's mother was much more interested in her future son-in-law. "Don't mind you father, dear," she'd said, making the sign of the pencil sharpener against her temples. "Tell me, this Jack Samuels of yours. Is he hung?"

"No, don't," she said. "I don't want to know, as long as he makes my little girl happy, I'm happy. My little girl. I can't believe my little girl is getting married. What do you need? Do you need a place to stay? A place to make your first little love nest away from home? Well, you can stay in the cottage, that's where you can stay. Your father and I want to help you two lovebirds in any way we can. Oh, there's nothing like young love. Don't you think the cottage is absolutely perfect? What's his father like, is he hung? Of course you'll have to get married in Texas, without his father's permission, I mean. I wonder why he can't get his father's permission? Just think, Romeo wasn't eighteen either, isn't it romantic? You'll have to take the VW. I'll go with you. We'll drive to Texas. You don't need your parents' permission in Texas. Did he pass?"

"Did he pass what, Mother?"

"Did he pass his physical, darling. You know, I mean has he ever had syphilis. This Jack Samuels of yours?"

· 30 ·

BILLY DAWSON WAS STILL
tied into his hospital bed, still flat on his back and still
had a hundred tubes jammed into his nose, into his
arm, up his ass, and out his dick. He was tinky-tinkying
into a bottle and going nowhere pretty damn fast.
There were bottles dangling over his head that hung
from what looked like portable clothes racks and he was
all taped up like a Christmas present. He was dizzy, had
fuzzy vision and fuzzier speech.

In the past seventy-two hours, he had slept damn
near to seventy, as far as the prune-pussed nun could
make out. As he ate through his arm, as he pissed
through his tube.

When he woke this time, he figured it must be either

morning or afternoon, because it was bright. Damn bright, from the high-ceilinged window. . . . And he lay there getting used to it. It took awhile. The pressure was to shut them again. To slip out, but he wouldn't. He had wasted enough goddamn time in bed.

He shook his head and waited for his eyes to refocus normally and then the next hurdle were the balls and chains tying him down. He would start by forcing his lower parts around, to sort of loosen up the tension. That's what he'd do, but he didn't. He forced and he forced, but nothing eased. Nothing moved. It took him awhile to realize that nothing eased because he hadn't even been able to locate the necessary muscles, never mind to get them moving. He was a prisoner of his own weakness, and didn't that chap his ole rear. He relaxed and breathed a whole lot. He forced the breath low, to get maximum energy from it, like lifting weights. He lay there and concentrated on moving below the bad areas. After a while he moved his left foot. The whole thing. Toes and all. He began to feel hopeful. He concentrated on gathering enough momentum and then started a steady pushing. He had it figured—first the sternum, past the hurt to the lower back, through the pelvis, and under the hips down the thighs would do it. He worked at it, and worked at it some more. Meticulously, measuring each parcel of strength, and then sank back into the pillows and realized that still nothing had happened. That all the energy was in his mind. But by the time the flat-nosed Mex slid the evening food rack past his door, he had both arms undone and was only waiting for a clear coast to get to the strap on his legs. He began to feel the old Dawson blood flowing. It wouldn't be so damn long now. Once he was undone, he'd pick the old tubes out of him like ticks off a hound and be the hell out of there before the old twat knew what hit her. He started sitting and felt the pull of the needle in his right arm, so he pulled it out, tape and all, and let it bang against the wall next to the bed. Then he lay back exhausted and stared up at the acoustic tiles on the ceiling.

He leaned over and it hurt, so he made himself keep that position. He grunted and gritted but he held. Only after a while did he allow himself to goose around with the buckle and when finally the damn thing opened and his legs snapped apart with a jolt, he fell backward riddled with pain.

"Ah," he moaned, licking his salty lips, "now that's more like it. More like Billy Dawson, the old me." He lay on his back a long time, tried to breathe around the holes in his gut, and after a while was able to pull back the covers for the next step.

Under the white thing they had on him he could sense bandage, the smell of gauze, and the scabby muck under that, all yellow and oozy under its crust. He slid his legs out from under the covers one at a time. He went real slow because he hadn't come this far to screw up now. Little by fucking little he got them over the side of the bed, where he noticed they'd already faded the same color as the sheet. He let them dangle over the side awhile and rested.

Trini Lucero had stopped by or called twice a day

for three days, until he found out Billy was off the critical list, then he went home, took a peek at his new boarder through the keyhole, and got into his own bed with a can of El Paso's refritos and a copy of *Fountainhead*. A few minutes later his new roommate climbed up on a chair and watched him through the transom.

Trini knew anybody else would leave town, but where was he supposed to go? Home? On his belly, the way his sainted father had always predicted? Bad enough that *Viva Zapata* had brought shame on the heads of the Mexican aristocrats. Trini was lonely. The only thing he had for sure now was Mort Dralon and his Lucero Defense Committee. But it was two weeks since he'd seen him, and the gnawing truth was that Mort Dralon was missed.

He'd missed him at Frijolito, and he missed him now, nuisance value, and everything. Without Mort's constant badgering, what else did Trini have in his life?

He called the hospital for the last time and they said Billy was fine. They said he was making a remarkable recovery and had the constitution of a garbage disposal.

Little white driblets of sugar water drained out of the needle that had been jammed up Billy's arm. It splashed faintly down the side of the bed and against the cream-colored wall. Billy forced his weight over the side of the bed and insisted that his pale legs do their stuff, whereupon he pushed himself away from the bed he'd used as a crutch and immediately keeled over, almost splitting his head open on the stand holding the bottles. The penicillin, the sugar water, and some yellow stuff all dripped into his hair as he lay on the floor out cold, his ass end hanging out the back of the hospital nightie, his hair getting all sticky.

When he came to, he tried it again, this time resting on his hands and knees till he had enough equilibrium to make it up all the way to his feet. There was no question of giving up. He had made up his mind to find his pants and get himself out of that vulnerable position. But his gut began to sear and with pain, and then the shoulder the resident had said might be paralyzed forever.

Piss on the resident, Billy said. Nobody was paralyzing his shoulder.

When he got to the door frame, he waited till the dizziness passed, then for the emptiness to sound an all-clear through the long hospital hallway before waddling off to the right on his spindly legs. As he proceeded, he left little drops of piss behind, drops that fell from the tube he had forgotten was still jammed up his dick. Little drops of piss like Hansel and Gretel's breadcrumbs, making a path for the nun to follow. The same nun he'd cold-cocked the night they brought him in.

But the nun wasn't the only one to follow Billy's trail. Mr. and Mrs. Jack Samuels, who had just stepped off the elevator on their way to Dermatology, watched the ass end of Billy Dawson making its way down the hallway too. Amy was first. By this time the nun, who had run to get the attendant, was back, and with her was the biggest hypo Amy had ever seen. It scared her —Jack, though, stood aside and smiled a little as she gave it to him. He even savored the sensation of shock as the muscles of Billy's left cheek quivered just a little and he collapsed in the arms of the attendant.

"Come on," Jack called on his way to the skin clinic on account of his arms, "come on, chattel. What do you think I married you for in the first place?"

But Amy didn't come on. At least not right away. First she watched the attendant pick up the limp body of her almost-rapist number two and carry him back to his room. Then she followed behind at a discreet distance so she could make out the number on the door. Then, on the way back towards Dermatology, she passed a supply closet, reached in, and stole a nurse's uniform. Only then did she come on.

But Jack might have held Billy Dawson against her anyway.

· 31 ·

ACTUALLY, NOTHING ABOUT
her marriage had turned out as Amy had hoped. First,
and most of all, the old ringing down there, between
her ulva and vulva. Nothing touched it. On and on it
rang, as if the big looked-for honeymoon eve had never
happened. Way past and still. All the time now, interrupting everything. The radio, the alarm clock. Even
the sound of her own stomach rumbling. Especially the
big looked-for honeymoon eve itself. Amy and her girl-
friends had imagined the bride wearing a long satin
nightgown with forty-four covered buttons and forty-
four satin loopholes, which the poor love-crazed groom
tried desperately to disengage before he might possess
his bride, *his passion commingled with the tangle of*

her hair, just like *The Foxes of Harrow* and *Kitty,* which turned out nothing at all like the sudden jab of her husband's icepick, bolting her to the mattress.

"I tell you she's crying," her father whispered to her mother, pressing his ear to the wall that separated the main house from the cottage.

"She's not a child anymore," her mother said, and two days later they were looking for an apartment.

"Out into the world" was how Dell Collins had put it, but Dave knew what she meant. She meant out of earshot; they were all against him. Now they were kidnapping his oldest daughter, spitting on her belly, and tying her to the bed.

Actually, Jack Samuels was only spitting on his own arms, it just looked like he was spitting on Amy and she wasn't really tied down either, she just had to pretend she was, and not move when he went at it—not a thigh, not a nipple. That's the way he liked it, that's all. Eleven sharp, rain or shine, and she'd better just get used to it.

"For heaven's sake, David," Dell said. "Amy is almost eighteen years old. Old enough to be on her own, with a job, a sense of what it's like to earn a dollar in this world. She can quit school, or let that husband of hers support her. What? Are we supposed to encourage their infantile fantasies?" she asked him. "I'm asking you, David . . . I mean, can we?" And so, a week after her mother told them they could stay in the cottage forever, they were on their own. Amy quit school, got a job at a top secret pharmaceutical house as a roller skater. (The plant was so large she had to skate down and up the halls eight hours a day filling orders and keeping her mouth shut. Some of the prescription items eventually headed for the top secret bases where headaches were SOP, so it was all very hush-hush.) When she got back to the apartment in the evenings, her husband wasn't back yet, and half an hour after he'd done it, each and every evening at eleven sharp, he was gone, ostensibly to his job at Valley Gold as a milkman, but really back to Trini Lucero's, to his old room, where he usually had a whore and still thought Trini was Al Velásquez, even though he was getting suspicious.

After he was finished with his women, Jack would get up on his chair to watch Trini through the transom. Once he watched him eat five cans of cold tamales at one sitting, never getting out of bed, and holding a phone in his other hand. Jack didn't quite know what to make of the phone, to figure who he was calling or why, but he knew if he watched long enough it would pay off.

Then one Saturday morning Jack decided he'd been working too hard and needed a vacation. He took Amy's old high school babysitting money, bought himself a Honda, rolled a towel behind him for a buddy seat, and told Amy they were going to try her out and see what she could do.

"Who?" Amy asked him.

"Get on," he said, taking hold of her upper arm and squeezing so hard she got a great purple welt.

They had been riding north for almost four hours and he wouldn't even stop at a ladies' room, so by the time they'd passed Sante Fe (heading up toward

Espanola), she could feel the cold pee drip down the insides of her thighs. She held tightly to the smooth leather jacket in front of her, her husband? and tried to pin-point the moment she first knew something had gone awry.

He moved the hand controls up to seventy and the ringing between Amy's legs echoed over the wind with the steady insistence of a five o'clock switchboard. By this time she could feel the urine turning to an itchy crust down her legs. She wished she were dead, or at least alive. She wished her husband would ride off into the eye of a hurricane. Some help he'd turned out to be. And her father? She wished he hadn't spent so much of his life talking to dead men, leaving him so unable to put her out of her misery himself.

They left the town and moved into the mountains, with the Rio Grande rushing along their western flank.

Please, she begged him. Wetting the bed was a childhood trauma.

"She's really something, isn't she?" he answered her and opened her up all the way. When they turned off onto Canyon Road, Amy's anklets were soggy. The sun filtered down through the layers of pine needles and pinion nodules, and they climbed higher and higher, up into the woodlands overhanging the huge hole between the rocks, way down where the Rio Grande foamed and roared.

Up on the top where they were going was the bareback butte and on the way, only narrow passes on black-widow web threads. Stark drop-offs down into the river. Amy closed her eyes and thought about her almost-rapist number two, and how best to contact him, but she let her head fall slowly onto the back of her husband's jacket out of sheer exhaustion. He made no move to push it away and she felt a quick jab of adrenalin. She tried, without falling off, to massage her aching legs and even to hold in the bladder that felt like it was dropping out through her nether seven-piece orchestra.

The road narrowed and the rocks flew to either side of their little motorcycle wheels. Down below, the road got smaller and smaller, like candy licorice laces or baby snake tails. Heights made her dizzy, but speed thrilled him. He pressed down harder around the accelerator and the glistening leaves ran one into the next with a big blur, around her sick head. Her ears popped.

And then they stopped. Very fast, with no warning. He let the cycle fall over as she managed to get out of its way and run behind a boulder to pee and bury her underpants.

"I see you," he said.

She turned and found him half-hiding behind the same rock. He was scratching the insides of his arms furiously and looked at her with a dazzling smile, lit up by hundreds and hundreds of electrified teeth.

"Wanta push it over?"

He took her hand and made her skip around the rock with him.

"No, I mean it. Want to? It'd be fun."

Again she looked at him and saw how he could smile marvelously when he wanted something.

"Come on, don't be chicken, how much could it weigh?"

She looked at him and then at the rock. He was serious and the boulder must have weighed half a ton.

"Why?" she asked him.

He shrugged his shoulders and threw out his palms. "I don't know," he said. "Why not?

"We can watch it splash into the river," he said, and then he took hold of her bruise again and suddenly socked her on it, right in the middle. "I said come on, now move."

This is not it, Amy whispered to herself, and it never will be—I have to contact Holy Innocents' Hospital just as soon as I can.

"Again," he told her. "That wasn't nearly hard enough. This time let me really feel it."

"One, two, three," Jack said, and on three they really leaned into the rock. Then one, two, three again. And again. And when it still didn't budge, he closed up his mouth and narrowed his eyes. He didn't sock her again because he didn't have to, while way down below them, in a hidden copse off the road that wound up from the river like a long string of spit, Ron Harkness was on his knees siphoning off the last of Lester Newbauer's dick. Ron had brought Lester up to Taos for the day to try and make up to him for having lost his scholarship, his rocking chair, the only mother's milk that had ever agreed with his ulcer.

"Push, lady," Jack was saying to his wife, "what did you expect? You could live happily ever after just like in *The Ladies' Home Journal*?

"Harder," so she pushed and she sweated and she watched her husband with his sidewinder eyes and his putrefied arms that stank like a dirty icebox.

"I tell you she's crying," she'd thought she'd heard her father whisper to her mother. But all he ever said to her now was, "Say hello to Ronald Croonquist, Amaryllis. Ronald is my friend. He knows I wouldn't say anything like that."

"I am pushing," she moaned. I am pushing and married and lost. I am trying to remember the fellow who carried a big stick and promised me something besides boulders. If I don't get it soon I'm going to forget what it is. Goddamn it, I'm pushing so hard I hear oceans pounding on my brain. I am trying my best to knee this sandstone bastard up out of its thousand-year-old niche. I am trying, I really am. Don't ask me anymore. I really and truly am. . . .

Meanwhile, down in their hidden copse, Ron and Lester looked for new places to stick things into, with their soft white bodies that glowed in the dappled sun. Some places were covered with freckles, the napes of both their necks were prickly with stubby red hairs, and they panted like small newborn terriers with shaved pink bellies.

"This doesn't make any sense," Amy said.

"What I want is all the sense you need," her husband said. "And I want to throw the rock into the water.

"Come on, push. . . . You think I rode all the way up to Taos just to stand around breathing the altitude? Let's go, we haven't got all day." And then it moved. At least it might have, a hair. A little bit off its damp mouldy perch, so that very fast, before it could lean back again, Jack knuckled into Amy's back and together they shored it up, and held, while Ron Harkness and Lester Newbauer climbed back into the Hudson for the rest of the narrow climb up the dizzying road to the crest.

"Did I tell you? Let up now and you'll be the one to sail over the cliff down into the rushing white-eddied river. Either way," he said, showing her his winning smile, "I get my bang!" He closed up his fist and pulled it just before it hit her iridescent welt bulls-eye.

"Just keeping you honest," he told her. "So you don't try any funny business. Wait till I give you the signal."

Lester drove and Ron squeezed his eyelids together so he didn't have to look down and scare himself.

"Now!" he shouted.

"Now?" Amy could feel the grip of his eyes against her throat.

"Now," he said to make sure they gave it everything they had at exactly the same moment.

"Again!" And this time, as she beat her body desperately against the obdurate rock, it suddenly groaned. She could smell her husband's arms right through his sleeves, bandages and all. It groaned and barely rocked. They dug into it again and pushed and battered it with everything, getting down on their knees and digging until Amy's purple bruise spread over all her surfaces. But the boulder did move. It lurched up out of its nest and then rolled, lumbering down the incline toward the cliff's edge, knocking smaller rocks out of its way across the soft, needled cliff floor. Then, on the edge, it teetered. It hung, as if hesitating in mid-air, and then fell. Suddenly, plunging heavily over into the emptiness, ripping off a side of the path as it went. Cranking into an overhanging branch, splintering the air, breaking off pieces of sky. It fell all right, through road and canyon, right into the mighty Rio Grande.

"Yeah," Jack yelled, and suddenly yanked on Amy's arm, dragging her over to the edge with him so she could chronicle in her soul the great careening wake and know with the finality of a job inextricably *done* that she could always be next. "Watch," he commanded and she watched as the hunger in her turned to nausea . . . from layer of air to layer of road, she watched. As it fell, this Triassic gallstone, through the yawning gulf into the river by way of chasm, landslide, and holocaust. Then the arc of its path moved from the Rio Grande toward the road . . . , where she suddenly noticed for the very first time a silver-colored Hudson making its slow way around and around like a beetle around a honey pot.

"Sweet Jesus," Amy screamed.

"Holy Mary, Mother of God," while Jack hoped, cursing only the lack of his tape recorder, and crossing his fingers.

Not that either of them could tell from way up there for certain if it was a Hudson. Or that two bald lovers rode inside, at that moment absolutely ignorant of any imminent quietus. . . . All they knew for positive was if the car didn't quickly move either a little faster or a little slower, it was curtains. Amy began "Our Father," and Jack began to scratch away at his scabrous arms

so fast he got a hard-on. And then came the vibration.
. . . One enormous, overpowering, earth-pummeling vibration followed by great globs of silt that came up as if
blown out the back of a vacuum cleaner. No air, no
breath, nothing anywhere else. Not Amy's mother,
Dell, who had put them out into the street because
they couldn't live in her cottage forever, or Jack's father
and his passel of blue-tick pit bulls, nothing but the
sudden cessation of earth and sky and a crippled
wrong-way Icarus.

Amy could feel the skin under her eyes parch and
pull apart like old Kleenex. . . . And then a little tiny
silver figure of Winged Victory welded to the hood of a
silver-colored Hudson, pulling out of the darkness into
the light, as if nothing had almost done it in. . . . As if
Jack C. Samuels hadn't whispered, "Shit, just my luck,"
under his breath so even his wife Amy wouldn't know.

Headed up, in second, as innocent as newlyweds. . . .

"Guess what?" they said, the two bald men, all
excited, all out of breath. "Guess what? We looked up,
and there it was. . . ." And then they said, "No kidding," the charming young couple leaning against their
motorcycle. . . . "No kidding," and they all marveled
together, the four of them, at the bald men's narrow
escape, and at how it ever could have possibly happened.

Afterwards they had dinner *à quatre* at the Pink
Adobe, and by the end of the week Lester and Jack were
ass-hole buddies.

· 32 ·

WHILE IT WASN'T STRICTLY
true that Ashley's brother, Edgar, came all the way to
New Mexico just to see her, he did have to drive the
sixty miles out from the airport and then sixty back
again, which wasn't, he assured her, peanuts either.

"Hi, Edgar," Ashley said, shielding her eyes from the
sun when he knocked on her muddy door in his Bond
Street herringbone. "How are you?" But she didn't give
him either her cheek or hand because they'd never
been what you could call close. Which was OK with
Edgar, who couldn't imagine anyone, let alone his sister, living that way. Shelves and more shelves of metal
bookcases crowded with rotting newspaper articles and
volumes of astrophysics and metaphysics and *Art Ap-*

preciation Made Easy. No place to sit. No couch. A dirt floor and crumbling walls. His own sister was living like a nigger.

"You are getting out of here, Ashley," he said, gripping her arm so tightly he reminded her of Mort.

"Oh, Edgar," she said, "don't be so dramatic," and pulled away.

"I come all the way from a very important business conference and you tell me not to . . . what do you mean '*dramatic?*' "

"Do you want a glass of water?" The words "business conference" reminded her of the father she hadn't seen in about ten years. That's the sort of thing he always said.

Edgar glanced nervously at his Le Coultre, for a moment allowed himself the luxury of admiring it, and then turned to his older sister and said quietly, "My plane leaves at seven. I drove all the way out to your hell hole because of a letter in which you said, after a dearth of correspondence from you of, if you will remember, eleven years, no, let me finish. . . . Eleven years, and now you say if I do not come to rescue you immediately you will do something drastic. Now, Ashley, I don't want to know what you mean by the word '*dramatic,*' but I certainly didn't come 120 miles out of my way for a glass of water, which I wouldn't drink here, under these conditions, if I did. Are you packed?"

"For heaven's sake, Edgar, don't you ever just talk American? Packed? What do you mean, 'packed'?" She picked up the boy's tow truck and took it into the house.

"You're my brother, Edgar. Who was I supposed to write to? Packed. That's ridiculous. What do you expect me to do, move in with you and Alice? Put up a cot next to your glass coffee table?"

"I don't have it anymore, Beth took it with her."

"Do you want some?"

"I don't want anything, I just want you to start making sense. I haven't . . . You know in my position I don't have all the time in the world. Look, Ashley, oh God, you haven't changed one bit. You are . . . Ashley, I have a . . ."

"I know, I know . . . a business conference. I thought you worked for a shoe store."

"A combine, Ashley . . . I am vice president of the largest, oh never mind. . . ." He closed his eyes, then put a hanky down on a folding chair and sat. "How've you been? Alice sends her love. I saw Paula. . . . She's . . . goddamn it, Ashley." He jumped up. "What are you doing in a place like this? You weren't raised in this kind of filth. It's different for him." He gestured with his head, towards the door. "He's used to it." He ran out of breath and looked down at her swollen belly. "When is it due?"

He looked back to make sure the hanky was still on the chair and sat down again. She said something he didn't catch. He nodded. He looked at the thousands of vitamins she had crowding the center of the old door they used for a table. Alice was right, Ashley really was beyond help, he should have cabled instead of come. Dolomite, acerola, tochopherols, inistol, choline, PABA . . . High-potency brewers' yeast . . .

"For godsakes, Lee, if you spent as much effort on your outside as you did on your in . . . you'd be on the cover of *Vogue*. Look at you," he said. "Don't you even have a mirror in this place?"

"August," she said. He looked at her.

"It's due. You asked me when it . . ."

"Oh yes," Then silence. He searched for another subject. Something safe. Surely a blood brother and sister could, after eleven years come up with . . .

"Still collecting cards?" Her card collection was the only thing he'd ever remembered her caring anything about. The picture side of jokers, odd eights of spades, sixes of clubs . . . she never used to be without it. Stuffed into that old recipe box she'd decorated with flower petals. She must have had a thousand of them. . . . Horses, you wouldn't have imagined there'd be so many different pictures of horses on the back of so many decks of cards. Outdoor scenes, famous paintings, dogs, all-over patterns, and she'd have them out, day and night, cataloguing them, rubber-banding the separate categories together, taking them out again and ogling them. Even at sixteen she'd had them. *Blue Boy* and *Pinkie* . . . under the covers at night, with a flashlight, figuring out how many of what she'd trade some other kid, usually eleven or ten, for how many of something else. He'd seen her once give up eight bicyclists and a vase of flowers for one palomino and spend the rest of the day crowing at the marvelous coup she'd pulled off.

She answered him and then looked away. He leaned forward but she wouldn't repeat what she'd said.

"What?" he said. "Do you?" but she just got up to pour some buttermilk.

"Where's . . . ," and he shrugged and again indicated the door. She didn't have to answer him about the cards.

"How long'll he be gone?"

He meant Mort. Nobody in Ashley's family referred to the son of the Jewish grocery store by name.

She shrugged. "Mort? He's digging. With the boy. For potsherds," she said to her brother's look.

"Look, Ashley . . . I don't want to hear his name. I . . . for godsakes, Ashley, this is not a person you are married to, this is an animal. Now, you knew that when you insisted on running off like a Bohemian. This is nothing new," he bellowed. He started walking back and forth from one end of the sink to the other. "I've come all the way from Philadelphia, Ashley. I've come to help you start over. Damnit Ashley, let's keep this as impersonal as possible."

When they took their battle stations, her position was behind the door. She didn't really see how they could. Keep it impersonal.

She could just make out the end of her brother's jacket from behind the Chimayo blanket, the tips of his shoes from behind Mort's *Columbia Encyclopedia*. There was nothing to do but wait. She closed her eyes. Why should she tell him about her collection? What in his whole life had he ever done for her except drive sixty miles from the airport when he was on his way to Denver anyway.

She'd always remembered her brother looking like

the pink end of a tongue forever sticking out at her, and he hadn't changed much. Sure, she still collected cards, so what? Even the other day when she'd gone to pick up Mort from that Lester Newbauer's, she'd found a nine of diamonds under the rug with a pair of red-boned hunting dogs on the back, which, added to the others, gave her sixty-seven dogs altogether.

"Why?" her brother asked her suddenly. He'd moved off and was now hiding somewhere in the bedroom.

Why had she married him, and she'd said, "I was a good dancer. He asked me to dance. Why does anybody marry anybody?"

She heard her stomach growl and wasn't sure if she'd eaten lunch or not. Then she saw him coming, the large man holding both the box of broken pottery and the little boy's hand.

"Here they come," she whispered, and the next thing she realized, the plan seemed to be working. She was kneeling on her husband's legs, digging her knees into his thighs, and Edgar had somehow gotten Mort's arms pinned under his back. He was sitting on Mort's chest and trying with all his might to gouge out Mort's left eye, which wasn't exactly the way she'd pictured it when she first wrote. Why, she wanted to know, did they always end up thrashing around on the floor, sometimes Mort on top of somebody else, sometimes somebody else on top of Mort.

She could see that he'd been knocked out. Edgar must have hit him on the head very hard, very fast. She watched him, her garter snake brother, with a silly grin on his face, breathing very hard. He had his mouth open and kept saying, "How do you like it, fellah?" Hitting Mort's eye in the same place over and over. "Stop it, Gar, what are you doing? Why are you hitting him in the eye?" It wasn't funny. And the boy was screaming and she was darn sure it wasn't like this with everybody. The boy was kicking his uncle in the shins and was pulling his hair.

"Rhile. Stop it, Rhile, that's your Uncle Edgar from Philadelphia. Rhiley, don't pull hair. Pulling hair is a terrible thing to do," and pretty soon there was Molina, the Arroyo sheriff. She supposed everybody in town knew what was happening when the sheriff took Mort out in handcuffs. By that time the boy was almost hysterical and there wasn't anything she could do to calm him down, not even hot cocoa with marshmallows.

· 33 ·

the charges, the sheriff let Mort go. On the way home he
said, "I'm surprised at you, Ashley."

She looked the other way and made a face, which
he couldn't see because she was walking two steps
ahead of him.

"You shouldn't have done that, Ashley. It wasn't
nice."

Rhile called out, "Not nice, not nice," made up a little
dance to go with it and a song which he sang all the
way home.

When they got home, Mort faced his wife and said,
"Ashley . . . I've finally come to my senses." Then he
put the boy in the car, where he fell asleep on the back

seat, stripped Ashley naked, and took everything she owned with him, in a dufflebag, to make sure she'd be there when he got home.

"I'm going to finish what I started," he told her, blowing a kiss through the plastic window, after first barricading all the doors with chests of drawers, the icebox, and his hi-fi equipment.

When the storm hit with its full force, Mort was already in Albuquerque. He was banging on Trini Lucero's door to tell him, his crisis past, the Trinidad Lucero Defense Committee was once more at high tide. Ashley, though, naked, shivering, and alone, sat in the drafty house and wrote another letter with Mort's leaky Esterbrook.

"Dear Mother," she wrote. "How are you? I am not so good."

The house whistled around her, and the only thing she found to wrap herself up in was the blanket Mort forgot to take because it was out in the woodshed where Rhile had played Dr. Dolittle.

"It's for your own good," he'd said to her, unsnapping her training bra. "Some day you'll thank me I kept the family together. Some day you'll know I was right."

"No," Trini begged him, on the other end. "No," from under his bed. "America is a free country." Now that Mort Dralon was here, banging on the door with the strength of ten, Trini couldn't understand how he could have missed him. Nothing was worse, huddled there on his rag rug. Worse than the voice of the people come to haunt him.

"The name is Al Velásquez," he said. "Can't you see

by the name tag that Trini Lucero's already paid his debt to society?"

"Be not afraid, Trinidad, my good friend, Trinidad," Mort answered. "The Mexican-American shall slip through the needle of heaven easier even than the chosen."

He was happy. He was clean again. He rubbed his sore left eye and knew with a certainty that nothing would ever come between him and his mission again.

But it so happened that Jack Samuels was also home. He had one of his women with him and he turned to her and said, "Shut your box, bitch . . . I wonder what that's all about."

"It was nice seeing my brother," Ashley wrote, "after all these years, though it was not nice of him to try putting my husband's eye out. You are right, Mother, blood is much thicker than marriage."

Ashley looked down at the thick belly hanging over her thighs and wondered where she ought to mail the letter, or whether it would be safer to stuff it in a Carta Blanca bottle and throw it out the window. She wondered if Mort would come home before the wood ran out. She wondered what difference it would make if he never did.

She looked down at her wrist to see what time it was, but Mort had been typically thorough. When would she accept the fact that only at his side could she come into her own, and nowhere else? As his helpmeet, he'd said. That's when he'd even taken her Kotex belt.

"Sometimes you're so dumb," she'd said and sat on the mattress ticking to watch him.

"I have an obligation which can't wait for your hanky-panky. Can't wait . . . ," while she went into Rhile's room to wrap up in one of his blankets.

"Oh, no you don't, young lady," he'd said, which was when he took them too, forgetting the one in the woodshed perhaps only because of the long overdue Trinidad Lucero Defense Committee on his mind.

"I wrote this in jail," he told her, waving a piece of paper in the air. "As a matter of fact, I ought to thank you for opening my eyes."

"A Petition of Conscience," he said, "that's what I wrote. Something to live by, guide our actions by. Read it," he said, and left her a copy as he took off with the boy.

She sat on the bed watching the fire die down, ripping the paper into tiny little pieces and thinking about her sister Paula. The plastic windows blew back and forth.

"Love, Ashley," she wrote at the bottom of her letter and the storm got worse. She got up, went over to a corner, and slid her backbone down the side of the wall and listened to the bumping of the knobs. She wondered where her old lover was, if he would ever come again. Maybe carry her off into the raging sand. It surprised her to realize she didn't much care if he did. She could see that in a little while the wind would tear right through the plastic windows. That everything they owned would be picked up and carried away, and that if Mort had only left her another blanket maybe she would have tacked it up over the windows.

The fire glowed close to the hearth in a faint purple

distance, and finally the wind did break the window. She watched as it pulled one of the plastic dropcloths clean out of its staples and whipped back and forth in the fury with the sound of wet sheets on the line. The entire storm tore into the room, with the sand and the wind and the little bits of outside. But when it left, it carried with it whatever it found . . . Mort's precious paper. His books, his notes, his files, like so many Sabine women.

Ashley sat in the corner and watched his carefully annotated paper, "The Changing Temperatures of the Vagina of the Tsetse Fly," come apart at the binder. The *Sane Society* got picked up and torn, cover from dedication page. A hundred Tables of Contents got separated from their Indexes. Leonard Bernstein followed Korzybski, Hoyt's *New Cyclopedia of Practical Quotations,* and *The Information Please Almanac.* But Ashley only watched.

She was trying to add up the bibliographed time parcels that had come to be her life, collating them with the blood of her emptiness, and cross-indexing them all with the gradual stiffening of her flesh. Paper and more paper. The room became a salad bowl and inside tossed the lettuce of her life.

She began to plop her knees down on the grainy floor, feeling them form little suction cups as they hit and popped up again. She became so cold she numbed, and finally it stopped. The storm was over and Mort was as naked as she was, not that she cared.

She didn't care much one way or another about anything.

· 34 ·

JACK'S WHORE'S NAME WAS
Bonnie; her father was a senator and her mother had
always told her, "You get nothing for nothing in this
world." If a trick named Jack wanted to spit on her
belly button and tie her wrists to the bedsprings, he
was only one of the screwballs she balled for money.
Right now, he was fooling around with a little portable
tape recorder while some freak named Dralon stood out
in the hallway, reading from what he called a petition
of something.

"Nor, as men of conscience," he was saying, "do we
. . . can we allow ourselves the belief that either personal or political . . ."

In the other room, Bonnie couldn't see Trini put his

hands over his ears at the word *political* or cringe
when Mort said:

". . . Citizen of the state . . ."

After Trini cringed, he banged his forehead down on
his rag rug and tried to swallow his clenched fists.

"We, the undersigned," the voice continued, "with a
wish to further consider . . ."

"Get lost," Jack said to her, "gowan." But how could
she? She still had her arms tied and the ropes were
cutting into her wrists.

". . . further consider, with a view to the formulation
of statements relating to the downtrodden masses . . ."

"Masses" was the worst yet, for Trini.

"How much do you want?" he whispered. "You can
have it all . . . what's left of what I put into teacher's
retirement, the canceled check stubs of my old GI Bill.
The cleaning tickets for two jackets and a pair of pants.
. . . What is it you want of me?" Trini asked patheti-
cally.

But all Mort answered him was: ". . . democracy,
founded on the principles of freedom of thought,
speech, and conscience."

"I had a heck of a time finding you," he said and Jack
got it all down on the tape recorder. "How come the
name on the bell says Al Velásquez? Who's he?" he
asked, "come on, Trinidad, my friend. . . . Open the
door and let me give you my hand."

"I'll call the police," Trini whispered. "Don't you
know Mrs. Filichia, the landlady, is only waiting for
that one false move? Who will take me in? Yesterday's
traitor. I'll bet even Quisling's out on his ear somewhere

in the cold, and not only Filichia, what about Vallejos y Hijos, Carnecería-Grocería?" Wasn't one false move all spictown could afford, all his friends who stood by him this far but no further. . . .

"All right for you," Mort threatened. He peered out the hallway window to make sure the boy was still asleep on the back seat of the car, while inside Trini moaned again. How could he ever eat the Board of Education's shit if Mort Dralon didn't take his feet out of his mouth?

No Petition of Conscience now, he begged. Now, when he'd already begun a plan of his own. Already written and mailed out three copies of "Socrates: His Fate and His Future," the true unbiased story of his credo, including even his epitaph in case it became necessary to die for what he believed.

He had sent one to the *Herald*, who'd called him, "the worm in the apple of knowledge."

The second he had sent off to the Advisory Department of the Board of Educational Security, who had seen to the forfeiture of all future pension rights, and the last he had mailed off to David C. Collins, Legislative Guild Representative, who, in all this time, had never been home once to answer the phone.

Mort Dralon's Petition of Conscience could put the credo expressed in "Socrates: His Fate and His Future" in a very bad light. Somehow he would have to stop him. Nothing must interfere with his honest efforts to purify his position in the community. But right then and there he couldn't think what to do. While he thought, he pulled the pillow off the bed and placed it on his head where he lay, on his stomach, against the wall, under the springs.

Meanwhile Mort quoted from Ralph Waldo Emerson: "When the will is absolutely surrounded to moral sentiment, that is virtue," he intoned. And after Emerson, he quoted Dralon: "Man must shoulder the responsibilities resulting from commitment. I am committed, Trinidad, do you hear me?"

Trini didn't, not too well, with a pillow on his head, but Jack managed to get it all down all right. He still wasn't sure where this Petition of Conscience affair would lead him, but as the plot thickened, he became brazenly confident it would, in the end, go somewhere.

· 35 ·

ABOUT TWO WEEKS AFTER
the magazines started coming, Dave Collins received
the first of the strange letters. It was all about the plant-
ing of perennials, a subject in which he could not have
had any less interest, unless it was in fishing plugs, the
subject of the second, which read:

Pleased to report that Hawaiian Wiggler back in stock.
Your order of six with *red* skirts on way. However, we are
backlogged on Crazy *Ike* and are most anxious to offer in
its stead, either *Johnson* Silver Minnow or Tiny *Torpedo*
[*Red, Ike, Johnson,* and *Torpedo* all underlined].

"Eager to help catch you the big one," it closed, and
was signed: Ben Arnold, Sec'y: International Waters,
Suppliers of Sportsmen Everywhere.

Now if Dave hadn't known better, he would have sworn it sounded like some sort of code, but it wasn't until the third letter arrived that he began not only to hide under the bed, but while there, to speak in tongues. That one was sent to the school, was addressed to "The Legislative Guild Representative," and started out "Dear Comrade Collins," plus which, he could have sworn the envelope had been steamed open at least once.

Dear Comrade Collins,

In reference to your recent inquiry regarding our Stradivarius. We regret to inform you that the varnish you asked about is not yet dry. Furthermore, events lead us to believe that this particular varnish never will be.

Of course, should subsequent developments signify a change in this assessment, you will be immediately notified.

This time the word "never" was underlined, and again the letter was signed Ben Arnold, who, this time, was secretary of Music of the Spheres Corporation, Ltd.

Well, that was it for old Dave. He began visibly to separate limb from limb. All his spare time was used for hunting down new phone booths in his vain attempt to get his name off even one of the subversive mailing lists. He'd call first *The Worker* and get some drunk on the other end of the line, and then *Liberation* and speak to a very young pacifist with eyes that never blinked. They kept telling him it wasn't that simple to get your name off a mailing list, once the Addressograph punch got into its slots. . . . So Dave would run through the streets from drugstore to bowling alley making sure to use another phone booth each time. But they kept right on coming. . . . The magazines, the letters, and whoever was after him.

By the time he got the letter that had only numbers inside the envelope (numbers cut from newspapers and magazines and pasted to the paper with rubber cement), Dell had taken to leaving two trays outside his door at night, one for him and the other for Ronald Croonquist. Dr. Harkness said it was the only thing she could do short of locking him up, poor man, which Dell considered. But after all, she finally decided that while he was harmless and could still get it up, what the hell.

· 36 ·

JACK HAD PLENTY OF TIME
to keep meticulous track of his well-orchestrated scheme
because his wife Amy still thought he was out deliver-
ing for Valley Gold. But even still, in the past week
he had begun to feel harried, maybe the scent of Martin W. on his track, not that he could be absolutely
sure. But just to make sure there were no slip-ups, along
with his tape recordings, Jack bought himself a bound
ledger and began writing everything down. He had so
many strings to pull it was difficult to keep track.

He'd make it a point to stop by late in the afternoon
at Lester Newbauer's. They'd reminisce about their
meeting in the mountains. They'd talk about their hope
for the future, and Jack would remember to bring a fat

bag of Fritos and a quart of dago red, Lester never guessing Jack had ever been there before. Mostly they'd chew whatever rag Lester would drag out, Jack didn't care, as long as his new friend, the fag with the ulcer, ate and drank heartily. Jack would mostly just listen, hypnotized by Lester's pudgy hand reaching compulsively into the forbidden cellophane bag, licking the salt off his fingers, and washing the dregs down with wine.

It was time and money, coming every day without fail, but Jack felt somehow it would pay off in time. Ulcers, faulty kidneys, a couple of gallstones . . . something was bound to pan out.

But what he could expect from Lester was only small potatoes compared with the job Jack planned to do on Mort Dralon, author of the Petition of Conscience. He tracked him, this oversized Green Hornet, to the Canyon de Seco Public School, where, it seemed, he taught math, science, civics, economics, and, in the evenings, showed movies from Coronet Films on etiquette.

Jack had devoted a paragraph in his ledger to Lester, two to Mort, and on pages 4, 5, and 6, he had outlined his plans for Al Velásquez, alias Public Enemy Número Uno. After discovering Trini's real identity, his star boarder decided he would, in the end, crown his entire career by getting his landlord to agree to burn himself alive, downtown, at high noon, where his smouldering body would tie up traffic for hours.

In a way, everybody else's just deserts were nothing much when compared to Trini's. But the only detail

Jack had yet to work out was how he could get him to do it. He'd been working on it and was, he felt, getting closer, and if only Martin W. didn't show up suddenly and ruin everything, he was sure he'd do it yet.

But he worried, so the scabs on the insides of his arms grew bloodier and pussier than he'd ever seen them. His wife Amy had to change the sheet twice in one night. Before and after. This went on for two weeks, but when Jack found out about Socrates, Amy was able to sleep straight through. Jack's skin cleared overnight. His eyes glowed, and as she lay underneath him he even smiled at her.

· 37 ·

AMY, MEANWHILE, CALLED
Holy Innocents' Hospital every day, and every day they
told her her savior was still on the critical list. She'd
taken, in her ardor, to lighting candles at the local
Catholic church and did nothing, at home or away, but
think of him.

She told the hospital she was Billy's sister and Thursday, somebody at the switchboard said he was finally
doing nicely.

Her guts rushed up into her throat. She could hardly
lie there while her husband banged away at her as he
did every night like clockwork before leaving, a half-
hour later, when he thought she was asleep. The
thought of her Captain Henry made her thighs throb,

which terrified her. They couldn't throb. One small, imperceptible shiver was enough to throw her husband into a fit. He would lash out, jump up and down, stamp his feet, and yowl like a kid who couldn't find his marble sack. She was too worked up for all that emotion now. She'd force the soft flesh on the inside of her legs to lie still and play dead till he was through and gone.

The parallels between her own situation and that of Catherine Barkley and Captain Henry in *Farewell to Arms* seemed positively other-worldly. The way Catherine found *him* again after never expecting to. The same way Amy had found Billy. In a hospital. And especially the way Henry had begged Catherine for mouth-to-dick resuscitation, the way Billy would undoubtedly beg her. . . . She could hardly wait. She didn't think she could live until Jack was through. Finished pawing her, gone, with the door closed behind him, off to wherever it was he went, so she could pull on the starched nurse's uniform and draw dark seductive lines around her eyes. Her mind sought the haunting Hemingway: You're not well enough (or something), Catherine had breathed (huskily) into Captain Henry's ear when he begged her. Please, he had replied, I need you, I want you. . . . Please. Something like that. . . . He'd practically beseeched her. Three times she said it would be too much for him but on the fourth he was on top of her, the only thing between them, his bandages. . . . And so, she knew, soon, it would be with her and Billy Dawson. He would lie on her. He would stick it in and she would, after her endless wait, be free.

She brushed the mascara heavily onto the right lash and nervously began on the left.

But she was, she had to admit, not without apprehension. After all, could she so heartlessly go to her lover when her very own father was, at that very moment, talking to himself in tongues? As he had been all day, every day for a month, so that her poor longsuffering mother, unable to bear much more of it, had had him carted off in a strait jacket?

Her mother said it was because of all the magazines. Coming and coming. His condition becoming increasingly worse as the size of the mail deliveries grew in bulk. Her mother said not only was he now getting *The Daily Worker, Liberation,* and *I. F. Stone's Weekly,* but the *Jefferson School Catalogue, The New Republic,* and, what terrified him the most, *The Bulletin of University Professors.* As she slipped into her slip, Amy knew she should have gone to see her father at the Santa Clara Rest Home instead of satisfying her own selfish hungers by going, as she was, to Holy Innocents to see Billy Dawson.

"Magazines? What magazines?" she mused as she buttoned up the stolen nurse's uniform. She stood in front of the mirror and worried that she looked too much like a vanilla Fudgsicle. Oh, if only Billy Dawson had been *mensch* enough to rape her in the first place, she thought, her father might never had had to go to Santa Clara. . . . Everything might have been different. . . . She wouldn't have had to get married, quit school, or leave home. Her father would have had her to count on. To come between him and his magazines, oh, beloved Legislative Guild Representative. . . . She wouldn't have ended up a married virgin who still walked around without her lid blown off. And she certainly wouldn't now be crossing Central in the middle of the night, impersonating a nurse, playing with herself to the tune of *Farewell to Arms*, or walking into Holy Innocents where Their Lady kept a somnambulent watch over the emergency entrance.

Instead she got into the Personnel Only elevator with a green-skinned food handler and rode up: three, four . . . she counted the floors, secure in the knowledge that he didn't notice the stolen uniform held together in back with three safety pins, or the glint in her eye which, she'd been afraid, could blind. I'm coming, Captain Henry, she murmured and the man looked at her. He ran his tongue over his teeth, but not for the likes of him had she left her only father alone with his arms tied behind his back haranguing Ronald Croonquist. . . .

"I'm coming," she murmured again, as the little green man in the blue uniform got off the elevator making a sucking sound with his tongue. "Hold on," she breathed as the door shut behind him, "I'm coming so you can rip straight away into my privates, which are panting so heavily I can hardly manuever myself down the corridor without drowning. . . ."

Room 600, 603, 619 . . . by the time she found 608 she had to lean against the chipping green wall to calm down. Her adrenalin was breaking Olympic records, chasing the oxygen out of her veins, and the suspense was more than she could deal with . . . would he or wouldn't he? What, she wasn't sure. Recognize . . . want, remember her. . . . Would he even be able to, in his condition? . . . Enough. If Captain Henry rose to the occasion, so would Billy Dawson. She opened the door. He was sound asleep on his back with a shiny trickle of spit seeping out from the side of his half-open mouth, and somehow the vision of the Hemingway hero got away altogether, but it didn't really matter. She closed the door and stood there looking at him from various angles. Trying to see if he measured up to her memories. Her nighttime fantasy, tearing her clothes, biting her breasts, having her and having her till neither of them could have any more.

There was a railing around his bed like a baby's crib which presented a problem, but not an insoluble one. She brought a chair to the side of the bed and with trembling fingers began to unbutton the uniform she had just a half hour before buttoned up. She stepped up on the chair and over the side of the railing. Billy never moaned. Never moved. He just slept as she stood over him and watched, one leg on either side of his head. But he didn't open his eyes and instead she got the scent not only of his sleep and the trickle of spit, but the swabbing and the probing and the whole total belly wound, including dressings.

"This is it," she whispered into his eyes. "Wake up and claim what is rightfully yours, you saw me second." But he didn't wake up. He only groaned in his drugged sleep, so she had to fish through her uniform pocket for her trusty Ever-Ready, which she then shined in his eyes until he started awake as if Destiny had finally, at long last, caught up with him.

"Jeeezus!" he screamed as he saw her with the flashlight under her chin, dangling over him like Elsa Lancaster Frankenstein. He wiped the slobber off the side of his mouth with the back of his hand, but with the other, reached up to fend it off, whatever it was.

She fell to her knees over him and whispered, "Me! It's really me. We're together at last. . . ."

He braced his arms against his hips and her body sloshed over him right through the starch—soft, white, female, making him pull away as if he'd burned the palms of his hands on hot marshmallows. "Oh my Christ!" he moaned as a sudden depth charge of breast plopped straight into his eyes.

"Don't," he begged, and rang for the nun with the tweezed face, but it was useless. Amy had had the foresight to disconnect the button even before climbing the chair.

"Lie back and enjoy yourself," she promised, "because I'm not leaving without it." And again she tried covering his mouth with her marshmallows but he only thrashed around like a dying albatross, whipping his doomed voice box back and forth, "Get'r away from me for godsakes, get'r away from me."

"Don't talk," she said, exactly like Catherine Barkley. "Save your strength," but instead of Captain Henry, when she dangled her nipples around his face this time, he swung so fast his nose whipped them together with a splaat! "Yippee!" She lowered them a third time and pulled in and out on the cheeks of her ass. There wasn't one single part of her that Jack Samuels could have approved of while she reached for, fiddled, sucked, and urged Billy's mighty member, which, no matter what, lay there in its spongy coma. She slowed up. She reached down and pulled on it softly with the insides of her mouth, as if sucking the last drops of Italian ices out of the bottom of the little ribbed paper cup. Then she pulled with her fingers, her palms, her belly, and between her knockers. She rolled like bread dough, but still Billy's winker played deader than wilted lettuce (the skin from an old chicken's neck, a kid's rubber bathtub duck).

No matter what she did, Billy Dawson's winker wasn't buying any.

"I told you you had the wrong room."

"Fuck you," she said, "and I mean it. . . ."

She let down her hair and swept it over him like a silken broom.

She had her legs jammed up under him and was really going all out, but all Billy would do for encouragement was to whip his head from side to side and tighten up on his eyes.

"I can't," he told her, but she said, "Don't tell me *can't*. Not one more *can't*, not from anybody. I'm not going out the way I came. I won't, so save your breath.

"Save it!" and she clutched at the shoulders of his hospital nightgown as Billy Dawson saw fear for the first time in his life.

She opened the straps on his legs and wrestled him over on top of her. Maybe it was leverage he needed. The illusion that he was on top of it. She didn't even care if her legs dangled out the sides of the crib, one to each side. But still he lay there. Heavy and inert. No battle remained in him for anything, which left her only her last straw. . . . "Come on!" she yelled, "I want it, goddamnit, I really need it!" But in her other hand, just in case, she clutched the tongue depressor.

"Try!" she said again. But he only lay there shaking his head sadly.

"Can't you see it's no fucking use?" he moaned. "Look lady, I can't help you. I've fought the brave bulls, flown the high-flying jets, landed for godsakes where no one else would even dream there might be a field with a road through it like a garter snake. I've done my bit." He wept. From defeat and a little from gratitude, even though the fear he had searched for all his life came not on the wind of a silver bullet, from a gored belly or the smell of rotting umbilical cord, but instead with the starchy scent of a soprano with eyes like pistachio ice cream cones.

And still his manly weapon lay helpless. A sad little cruller, two days old and saturated with confectioner's sugar.

Amy had no other recourse. . . .

"Never mind," she said. . . . "There, there," and she carefully took his limp little weewee and guided it onto the tongue depressor like a sick worm on a doll's stretcher. Then she guided it into her throbbing tunnel with thumb and index finger. . . . At last, omigod. . . . At long, harrowing last.

"I want it," she moaned in anticipation, "and you do too," as little by little it slid in. "Hell," she said, "everybody wants it, you can't kid me. . . . I read the *Heptaméron* of Navarre at nine, the *Decameron* of Boccaccio at eight and a half."

O.K., he wanted it. But what did wanting have to do . . . You couldn't call Cincinnati on a nickel anymore, either.

"No," she screamed, "be careful or it'll fall out. I've come a long way," she bellowed down his eyes, "and this time is it." It, it, it, as it lay there, Billy's garlic blood sausage, as soft and gooshy inside her as an eclair. And then he struck.

Not Billy.

Her savior, in husband's clothing.

Perhaps from the corridor. Perhaps from the fire escape. Perhaps on the wings of song along with Peter Pan . . . Jack Samuels with his right hand deep down into his pocket.

"Oh God," his wife had just bellowed. "Oh God, do something, I can't stand any more." So he did. He brought his hand out of his pocket and with it came a half-worn bar of Ivory soap which he very hard and very fast jammed up the crack in Billy Dawson's ass (Billy's tassle still up Amy's tootie). He jammed it way in, pluking him so purely his little weewee stiffened harder than an obelisk. High. Up and *in. In Amy's very spot.* So that her frantic little belltower started in ringing, louder, clearer, and jazzier than even she had imagined.

"I did it!" she moaned before biting her tongue with joy. "Goddamn Holy Virgin of us all, I did it after all. . . ." Which was nothing compared to the enthusiasm of Billy, who, with a little help from Procter & Gamble, let himself jerk off into one helluva double-edged oblivion. . . .

· 38 ·

BUT JACK SAMUELS WAS
only beginning to act. Trini, too, was feeling the pressure. As his boarder so eloquently put it to him, what
other choice did he have? Even he could see that The
Herald had no intention of printing "Socrates: His Fate
and His Future" as it would, Jack explained, too obviously vindicate him and indict them for libel or at
least defamation of patriotism. The Legislative Guild
Representative, he'd heard, was taking the waters and
would never have answered the phone anyway, and
worst of all, though he hated to admit it . . . now that
the fickle public had other hides to fry, his name was
hardly, if ever, mentioned even in the gossip columns.

It was quite, quite clear. He did, indeed, have no other choice.

Though he still, morbidly, bought the paper daily, read voraciously down one column and up another in hopes, in vain hopes, finding out only of a Quisling named Ed Thiessen from Moline, Illinois, who had been caught stealing *Our Glorious Brothers* from the Fairlawn branch of the library, of a nine-year-old girl who had stood up before the entire sixth grade to say that she wouldn't dream of accepting the DAR medal for perfect attendance even if it were offered her because, as she put it, "Tomorrow belongs to everybody, even undesirables." And then one day Trini read of Morton Dralon, which, it surprised him to learn, brought a lump to his throat.

No, Jack Samuels was perfectly right, his story would never be known if he refused to burn himself alive, downtown at high noon, so his body would tie up traffic for hours. He would slip into a premature grave a totally forgotten traitor. Whereas. Whereas, if he did burn himself to a cinder, he could at least stand before them and read from "Socrates and His Future." Then after he went, they would at least understand.

· 39 ·

played with his fingers, his notebook lying next to him.
He moved his fingers so fast and so furiously, right up
next to his eyes that no one but his old psychiatrist Dr.
Gershorn would know he was not silently practicing
either the *Allegro ma non tanto* from the Sibelius violin
concerto, or the Paganini *Caprices*.

But Dr. Gershorn would have recognized the frantic
movements for another sign, even without the notebook. To Dr. Gershorn they would have meant that his
old patient was close, practically breathing down the
neck, of whatever scheme he was up to. But then
Gershorn had had a lot of experience with Jack's
habits.

The book was open to "Things to Do."

Mort Dralon's name was written under the title and crossed out. Under Mort's crossed-out name Jack had written: "Killing a praying mantis carries with it a twenty-dollar fine."

Then, under the sentence about the praying mantis, he'd written Dave Collins's name. It had been crossed out, too. Under Dave's name he'd written: "Dogs have cold noses."

Next came Ronald Harkness, Psychological Counseling; Lester Newbauer, ulcer; his mother-in-law, Dell Collins; his wife (name crossed out); and finally Trini Lucero.

It wasn't clear whether he ever knew Billy Dawson's name. At any rate, it did not appear anywhere in the pages of his ledger.

Under all these names he had written: "The varnish on the Stradivarius is not yet dry," and he had underlined the word *not*. First he had underlined the word *varnish*, but had apparently changed his mind. Had Dr. Gershorn had a chance to look at Jack's new bound ledger, he would have had a lot to say. But, he didn't.

After finishing his finger exercise, Jack felt so relaxed he fell asleep. His wife hadn't been home for three days, but he never even wondered where she was. He was so pleased that the sores on the insides of his arms had cleared up, he never even thought about her.

· 40 ·

TEN MINUTES AFTER THE
principal received Jack Samuels' tape of Mort reading
from his Petition of Conscience, he called Mort into his
office and fired him. He said twenty minutes was all he'd
give Mort to clear his undermining ass out of there and
then turned his back. As the ax fell, Mort's eyes filled
with gratitude. A mantle of self-righteous indignation
poured deliciously over his shoulder pads like a Pond's
rubdown. So thrilled was Mort with his sentencing that
he sank to his knees and kissed the principal's ring
finger. Always the second pirate, never the Red Shadow,
Mort had finally become his own notorized martyr.

So marvelously indignant was he (upon leaving the
scene of his mortification, to tell his wife and child) that

he never even noticed the absence of the Pontiac. And it wasn't until a good five minutes after he had surveyed the wreckage of his home that he realized his wife's latest act of vengeance made this same martyrdom a mere jot on his tittle.

He stood there . . . in the middle of his now destroyed castle and loosened the bolo from around his neck. Small salty tears trickled down his apple-rosy cheeks. Mort Dralon even smote his breast.

"Darnit!!" he cursed. . . .

"How could she do this to me?" Was everything he held near and dear to be foully ripped from his bosom? Was there no warm corner left to him anywhere? He sat on the broken card table and read Ashley's note, but when he came to the word "divorce," he rose unsteadily to his feet.

Divorce? After five deeply satisfying years and almost two deeply satisfying children? How could she speak of divorce? The last dregs of his mortification in the principal's office turned as tasteless as stale Double Bubble. He sank to his knees amidst the clutter of amputated lumberjack shirts and disembowled bus driver's pants, and finger his Funk and Wagnalls, chewed by Rhile's gerbil. In his other hand he fondled the *Grand Canyon Suite* by the Boston Pops, which had been warped in the oven. His hi-fi needle lay blunted next to the knife sharpener, and the punch lines from his favorite "The Most Unforgettable Character I've Ever Known" had been thrown mercilessly in the sour foam forced out of three shaken cases of opened bottles of Cours. What was left to him . . . ? His life's work gone in the sandstorm, the order of his everyday universe in hopeless disarray, his perfect record as a teacher of math and science . . . and now his wife and seeds. . . .

Mort smelled the aroma of his mother-in-law, Thalia Clukis, and his heart was heavy. Her fingerprints became more and more in evidence in the vindictive rummage left to him from his life. "Oh woe," he cried and then found the crumpled slip of paper with the Taos telephone exchange scribbled in Ashley's hand. "Aha!" he quoth, immediately revitalized, "if they think they've seen the last of Mort Dralon, martyr, cuckold, wounded beast, they have quite the wrong Williamsburg kike in mind. . . ."

Meanwhile, in a Taos motel, wearing her mother's sweater, because everything she had ever owned Mort had somehow not only stolen but lost, Ashley was thinking the same thing. She shuddered.

"For godsakes, Ashley," her mother said. "That's vicuña."

"Sorry." Ashley tried to sit up straighter. But she wondered. Vicuña? What's vicuña? And why does she always look at me as if I were somebody's cast-off overcoat? She tried to make her shoulders go the other way, leave the seams of her mother's sweater alone, but it wasn't her fault she weighed more. She was healthier, that was all. And she watched her mother force her attention into the binoculars so Thalia didn't have to look at her anymore.

Not that Thalia expected her stumbling son-in-law to have the vaguest idea where to look for them. She shook her head quickly to dispel that old gnaw of hers. Goway, she told it, the thought up her ass. With all that size on him, and a Jew to boot, there must have been something her daughter had seen in him. It surprised her to realize that even after all those years, she still wondered if it wasn't all in his fly. No, she shook her head quickly again. He was a slob, and who cared how big it was, and how hard it would feel if they ever did get together.

Again Ashley leaned over, and again the seams on the sweater stretched. Had there been any decent way out, Thalia wouldn't have dreamed of coming all the way down here to her daughter's purgatory. But she was, after all, the girl's mother. . . . How would it look? Though why, she absolutely could never figure, if she had had to marry a Hebrew, couldn't he have at least been in banking?

She ran a distracted hand over her grandson, who lay in the other bed, assured herself in the mirror that she didn't look old enough, grimaced slightly because the child was more Jew than Tyler, and thought, with a giggle, of how they had told the boy, of course his daddy wanted him to open all the beer in the fridge and to shake it all over the chicken, which wasn't half what the Hebe deserved for running off with a girl with Ashley's pedigree in the first place.

Then she looked at her daughter stretching the beautiful vicuña again and thought she was going to be ill.

· 41 ·

for Albuquerque, Mort hitched a ride to Dallas Motors and told them he just wanted to take the little Ford around the block to see what she was made of. He even got them to check the gas and oil.

"No sign of him, Ashley dear," Thalia said. "Relax." After all, relaxing was the only thing which just might possibly save the sweater.

"Is Daddy coming, Mommy?"

"No, Rhile, go to sleep, Daddy isn't coming." . . . Except that he was. He turned off Central as soon as he got out of Dallas Motors' sight and instead of taking the little Ford around the corner, headed it up Route 54, straight towards the Ye Olde Weste Motel, just outside of Ranchos.

Too bad, Ashley thought, her mother couldn't have chipped in even a few dollars for another room. It would have been so much easier for the boy to fall asleep. Not that she didn't appreciate how difficult it was to have to go all the way around the world every year on a shoestring . . . or the many other sacrifices her mother made. . . .

"Why?"

"Why what?"

"Why isn't Daddy coming?"

"Your daddy isn't coming because your daddy wasn't invited, Rhile, now go to sleep."

"I will, Gramma. Don't worry, I'll go to sleep."

"I'm not worrying." And Ashley marveled at how easily her mother managed him. She seemed to have such a knack.

Outside the low vegas pushed through the heavy adobe and left fancy shadows in the moonlight.

The hair on Ashley's arm stood straight up, and it couldn't have been that she sensed Mort on his way because he hadn't even hit Santa Fe yet.

The sign said Ye Olde Weste Motel, but it had once been the Vigil spread. Sheep. All the way from Canyon del Muerto to Jemez. She read that on the little folder next to the bed. But all Ashley knew was there she was, away from Mort at last, and yet not really away either.

They had camouflaged the Pontiac with the overhanging night pinion and it was primed for a fast getaway. It had a new lock and a full tank. If all went well (she crossed her fingers), Ashley Dralon would soon be somewhere else. She didn't care where. A new start, her mother promised her. "You deserve it."

Yes, all in all, Thalia Clukis was pretty pleased with herself. It wasn't every mother who would come all that distance just to give her daughter a second chance when she'd told her so in the first place. And at that moment, right outside of Espanola, Mort Dralon stopped at an Amoco station to find out what it was that made the steam rise up from the radiator and fog the windshield.

Every so often Rhile thrashed about. "Why isn't Daddy coming?" he said into his pillow. And then he'd whispered, "Daddy is too coming."

Ashley had wanted to head straight off for Philly. But Thalia said, "For godsakes, to come halfway around the world and miss Taos? Don't be an ass, Ashley, dear."

Every once in a while Ashley would look at her. At the ruby and gold snake that writhed up her mother's arm. At her small veiny feet. Mother, she said to herself. A word like any other. Mother, rolling the sounds around her tongue. You. Female. Seductress. She lay against the wall. In the morning and on the next mornings it would be easier, she told herself. Then. Then she would be able to say:

"I'm leaving, going away, not going to be here anymore," and it would mean something. Then . . . it got later and quieter. After a time she told herself she *was* going away, she really was, but she felt her head shake. Her head said, "No, you're not. Never. You're never going any place," and her head knew better than she did. Because in a little while she heard somebody call:

"Ashley, I know you're in there," and she knew that the whole time she had been sitting in there, stretching her mother's sweater, she'd been waiting for it.

"I know you're in there." And her mother said, "Don't answer him. Shhh," her mother said.

"I'm coming in, Lee. Might as well open up," but she did like her mother said, except she whispered, "Uh huh," from habit. "Uh huh," she said, because that's what she always said when he spoke. Then Thalia whispered, "Jesus! He thinks he's Superman." She motioned for Ashley to peek through the blinds and then said, "There's not a judge in the world would pronounce him sane," as he stood straddling the eight-foot adobe wall, with his hands out to the side as if he were grabbing the stars for balance. But when Ashley looked, all she could see was her past and future silhouetted in front of a lover's moon with no glow.

And the road was a ribbon of moonlight,
And the barrel beneath her breast,
And Morton Milton Dralon came riding, riding, riding endlessly after her.

"Ashley!" he called again, and the little boy said, on his knees, "See, Mommy, I told you Daddy was coming," and he called out, "Daddy!" And Mort called out, "Rhile!" And Mort sobbed, and said, "Son!" And Thalia called the police. And Mort said, "Son," again. And then he said, "Home, let's go home, son. Tell your mother to come home!"

"Mommy, Daddy says . . ."

"Now, Rhile, you just tell your father that I am divorcing him. Look, Mort," she said. "It happens, read the paper. You just put an ad in the personals. I've read them. About not being responsible."

"Open the door, Ashley!" calling through cupped hands, so tenuously balanced up there she wondered to herself if she ought to hope he would fall or wouldn't fall. Because. If he fell, would she be the one to have to mend the rip?

"Let's talk," he said.

"Mommy, Daddy said . . ." and when she sneezed, he said, "I know you're in there, Ashley. I recognize the sneeze." So Thalia said, "Look, talk to him. Keep him busy. I'll take the boy out the back way."

"There's Daddy, Gramma. . . ."

"Plan B," she said. "We'll put plan B into action—you remember plan . . ."

"Uh huh," Ashley said.

"Concentrate, dear. I've come all the way around the world for this moment," and Mort out in moonlight was a cardboard portrait, two bits a cut on the boardwalk at Atlantic City, calling out: *My seed! My issue!!*"

"Rhile," he called and windows began to slam.

And somebody next door hollered, "What's the matter with you? There are decent people in here trying to sleep!"

And Rhile said, "It's Daddy. Mommy, it's Daddy! Daddy'll freeze to death, Mommy, Mommy, he has to make, Mommy!"

And finally Mort was feeling around outside the window and trying to force it open, which Ashley just couldn't understand. "Why!" she kept on saying. "Everybody knows it's better for the child to be with the mother."

"Look, Mort," she said. "It's better for the child to be with the mother! I read it—" He had the window up and was already sticking his big hairy head through.

"They fired me!" he shouted. "Ashley, do you hear me, they fired me!" While his son ran towards him in terror, with his mother close behind him.

"Cross my heart," Mort cried. "Isn't it wonderful? They actually fired me! I am a victim of political persecution at last," and he grabbed Rhile by an arm and drew him towards him. Ashley, who tried to brush Mort's arm off, grabbed Rhile by his other one.

"If you'll just go," she said, "we will be on our way, Morton. . . ." She tried to keep her voice very calm and her words very distinct.

"I tell you, they fired me, Ashley, didn't you hear me?"

"That's nice," she said. "But I am the boy's mother, you know. I have a right to . . ."

But Mort didn't hear to what. For his hopes were noisily being dashed against the small, ragged fragments of his heart.

No, he wouldn't let go of his half. The boy was half his. He had no intention of letting go of his half, and if Ashley didn't care a fig whether or not he got fired in these perilous times, why should he?

"Don't be asinine, you two," Thalia said, but why should Ashley be the one to let go? It was better for the child to be with the mother, that much Ashley was sure of. She'd read it in a lot of different articles.

So Mort pulled quietly on his arm and Ashley on hers, while the boy told them both, very quietly, "You're hurting me."

"You're hurting him," Mort said. Making Ashley say, "No, Mort, *you're* hurting him." And it only made her pull all the more, Mort too. But pretty soon Rhile didn't even cry anymore. He was so busy peeing in his pants.

Boy, he peed so much, the flannel of his pajamas stuck to his leg like a mustard plaster. Still Daddy wouldn't let go.

"Daddy needs you."

Or Mommy either.

"Mommy will buy you bubble gum just this once."

And then Daddy some more, and Mommy some more.

"Come home," Mort said. "There is a stand that must be taken."

"Everybody else gets divorced," Ashley said. "Why can't I?"

And after a while one of them heard a clicking. And when they both let go at the same time, the little boy fell into a wet heap with one arm hanging there kind of funny, and Thalia Clukis said to her daughter: "I told you to be careful. How many times do I have to tell you, that sweater is vicuña!"

· 42 ·

BY 11:09, RON HARKNESS'S
11:00 to 11:45 still hadn't said anything, so he very
quietly flipped once more to his appointment calendar.
Jack Samuels at 2:00. He knew the name, and for some
reason it disturbed him. Jack Samuels? He was sure he
knew the name . . . while his 11:00 to 11:45 fussed with
her skirts, lay like a rock, hands folded on her snatch.

He leaned back as still as a tiptoe so he could agonize
about Lester without her finding out. Lester and the
old crowd hanging around again and all his other dis-
orderly habits. It was a good thing they'd be going to
Chaco that weekend. . . . Give him a chance to talk to
him, knock some sense into his head . . . all those
leeches sucking away at his very life's blood, if you

gave them half an inch. . . . Just because Lester had nothing else to fall back on.

"My father wore green socks," she said. "That's funny, I never remembered that until just this very minute."

"Green socks?"

"I mean it, not until just this minute. Isn't that interesting?"

Again he thought of the name, Jack Samuels. "Very. It's very interesting."

"And green ties, too, come to think of it."

"You don't say."

"Funny how you can forget a detail like that, I mean it's hardly that I don't remember my own father; my God, a man like that. . . . But green is a funny color. I mean, he even wore green underwear. . . ."

Maybe he could rearrange his Monday appointments, give them a little longer holiday.

"You're not listening to me, Doctor."

"Of course I'm listening to you, Mrs. Collins, what makes you think . . ."

"O.K., if you're so smart, what about his jockstrap?"

"Whose jockstrap?"

"I told you, you weren't listening."

For a while, then, there was silence. Dell Collins, Ron's 11 to 11:45, had had her feelings hurt. After all, if her own doctor wasn't interested in the fact her father had even his Q-tips dyed green, what proof was there he listened to her about Ronald Croonquist, about the discouragement of visiting her husband in the mental ward of the Santa Clara Rest Home?

And then there was Grottewit at 11:50, who broke

into hives at the sight of Ovaltine, and then Salazar, at twenty of, who wore high-gloss nail polish on his toenails, under white sweatsocks and steel-toed electrician's boots. For lunch, Ron had salmon on toast, and not for one minute did he stop worrying about Lester, who'd gone nothing but downhill since losing his scholarship, or this Jack Samuels, whom he knew he knew. But from where?

"Well, well, well," he finally said, when two o'clock rolled around. "So you're Jack Samuels, how've you been?"

"Doctor," Jack answered, staring at his knees, "I can't tell you how pleased I am to be here. I, I, . . ."

"Never mind," Ron said, "I understand. Please lie down."

"A pleasure," and after a while Jack had his legs crossed on Ron's couch and was deep into his biography, with his eyes closed.

"My father died when I was one," he began. "He left my mother with thirteen children, twelve girls and me." He told Ron his mother had a clubfoot and had sent all the girls through Wellesley on money earned scrubbing floors. He then admitted to a fear of red fireplugs while he listened to the whirring of somebody else's tape recorder for a change. He said he was afraid of small dogs with soft fur, old-fashioned baby carriages, and merry-go-rounds. He said he also had a complex about red canoe paddles, lemon Jell-o, flowered rugs, bike spokes, and pearl earrings.

"Aha," Ron said. "Pearl earrings?" and quickly turned off the tape, pressed *rewind*, and turned it over.

But as soon as he did, Jack took the opportunity to sit up straight, and say with an unnaturally loud voice: "What are you doing, Doctor? Doctor???? My goodness, Doctor," he screamed, "you can't do that!"

Ron looked up in amazement. . . . He watched Jack Samuels start to rip off his clothes. . . .

"Take your hands off me," Jack shouted. "Dr. Harkness!!!" and as Ron watched there were Jack's things, all around him in great wads. And then this Jack Samuels put his palms to his mouth and screamed through them, "*Rape!!!*" at the top of his voice.

But Ron still wasn't connecting. He still had one finger pressed on the *rewind* button and the other held in front of his mouth, "Shhhh. What's the matter?" he said, but he kept looking at the tape recorder and watching the spinning reel.

So Jack screamed, "*Rape!*" again. And this time he got up and made a whole lot of noise. He knocked over a table and ran by the door and banged on it, locking it at the same time, because he had waited till he'd heard noises in the waiting room and knew there were witnesses. Then he scratched down his cheek with his nails. . . . "Help!" he yelled. And then, as Ron came to with an unbelieving jolt, Jack burst out into the outer office bellowing like a virgin. Richtmeyer, Ron's two fifty, clutched at her skirts. She was huddled up on the couch in the corner with a sad look on her face. . . .

"I'm a happily married man," Jack screamed, as he ran by her, with Ron right behind. He paused, unsure of whether to chase Jack down the stairs or not. Maybe he should stay with Mrs. Ackerman. No, not Mrs.

Ackerman . . . "I can explain everything." Mrs. Ackerman was three twenty. This was Mrs. . . . Mrs. . . .
damn, it was on the tip of his tongue as he ran on down
the stairs past his brand new shingle, *Family Counsel-
ing/Individuals/Groups/Hrs. By Appointment,* and up
the street, across the front of the bowling alley and into
Lomas, with the cars and the red lights and that mad-
man, still screaming, *"Rape,"* looking hysterical, pointing a finger at him, and in one afternoon ruining everything. . . .

· 43 ·

JACK CALLED HIS MOTHER-in-law and said he had to talk to her. "About Amy," he said, but it turned out Dell Collins didn't even know the girl was missing.

He said he had to change first because his clothes were a mess.

"Oh, don't stand on ceremony with me," Dell said, but Jack said, no, he meant it, his clothes really were a mess. Which was true, because he had written down Dell's name in "Things to Do" right after Ronald Harkness, Ph.D. (now crossed out). The last he'd seen of Ron Harkness, he had two police cars after him and was jumping over a kids' teeter-totter in a shopping center playground.

He told her he would be over in half an hour, and for some reason, after he hung up, Dell found herself putting perfume down in between her breasts and slipping into something a little more accessible.

· 44 ·

JACK HAD A LOT TO DO BE-
fore disposing of his mother-in-law. First of all, and
most important of all, there was Trini Lucero, and he
didn't want to miss one minute of his landlord's final
summing-up before he burned himself at the stake in
front of Penney's.

He hurried crosstown on Bernalillo, cut down Coal
and got a parking place right across from the *Watch-
tower* lady busy saving souls on the corner of Fifth and
Central. But, when he parked, got out the tape recorder, and set himself up for the kill, he could see
things were not proceeding exactly as he'd promised
Trini.

Sure, he'd told him, why won't they listen? It's not

every day the carnivorous public gets to hear a sacrificial lamb speak out in his own behalf.

Promising Trini a willing audience before he did
away with himself was Jack's trump, but the audience
just wasn't cooperating. They were crossing over to get
to the sales at Fedway's. They were having themselves
enchiladas in the Court Cafe . . . they were taking their
sneakers into Menaul's for new soles and heels, but
they weren't paying any attention to Trini, up on top of
a midnight blue Kaiser, in his gasoline-soaked suit,
sparkling in the sun, telling how it was to be misunder-
stood from the heart.

"For such as Socrates comes to rent asunder!" Trini
was quoting, at the same time bringing his right fist
down hard into his left palm (*The Beginner's Guide to
Public Speaking*'s guaranteed gesture for *intensity*).

"Be not fooled," he decided to say next, and to ac-
company it with the standard gesture for *supplication*
(bringing both palms together and tilting the head a
bit heavenward). Both sentiment and gesture used
previously with such success at old Alameda High . . .
but still they passed him by.

"Orate to your heart's content," Jack had told him.
"Orate till your tongue falls out, just don't spit on the
matches!"

But what good had his oration done?

What points had he secured?

The minute they realized who he was, up there on
the midnight blue Kaiser, they said, "Hoo hah, Pontius
Lucero, the Mexican Antichrist. . . ." Some of them
even threw Crayolas as they passed, and one lady, who

didn't have any crayons, swore if he wasn't burnt to a crisp by the time she'd had her lunch, she'd bring buns and fry him herself.

Oh, they'd stop long enough to curse at him, but they just weren't interested in the case against Socrates. Jack could see it was discouraging Trini. That the burning desire to vindicate himself before their eyes as a preamble to burning himself alive was dwindling with every forensic gesture.

"Stop!" Jack spoke at them as they moved on by. "Stop!" as they went into Hinkley's, Sears, and even up to the army recruiter, who sat at a card table with an American flag in front of the gas company.

But that wasn't the worst. The worst was that somebody up the street did have a crowd. . . . The biggest goddamned crowd Jack had ever seen, and it didn't have anything to do with Trini.

He worried that Trini had seen it too, up there on the Kaiser, where he had a terrific view, as he implored his nonexistent audience—fists in the air (to express consummate *commitment*)—for attention, so he could at least tell them, "there is a dry rot spreading through the grass roots of the nation like a ringworm." Jack was really worried that if Trini saw the crowd and heard the hoopla up there at the other end of town, he might give up all together. And then he saw a little old Navajo lady with Chimayo blankets over her arms and thunderbird necklaces around her neck go up to Trini and ask him something.

It gave him heart. It might not have had he known all she wanted to know was whether Trini wanted to buy a small *ojo de Dios*. Maybe a genuine Indian ring for a loved one?

"I tell you, the moral fiber of the nation is being eroded right out from under us," Trini bellowed over the sirens on their way down the street to see what was going on. And even the Kotex saleman in cowboy boots who'd stopped to scratch his athlete's foot, the lone lady in a purple snood, and a kid in a satin roller-skating jacket, who screamed, "Come on, Pancho, get to the fireworks," hurried off. The sirens were more than even they could resist.

"The kid's right," Jack screamed at him. One clean flame would bring them all running. "Screw that upstager up the street, let's get to the action Lucero!!!"

But still the traffic was backed up as far as the Roxy, and even Jack couldn't stand it anymore.

"I stand before you a repentant sinner!" Trini screamed as Jack shook his head and knew all was lost.

Trini moaned. The mob down the block was so loud, the noise of triumph so deafening, he couldn't even hear the chirping of his own bowels.

He turned to Jack Samuels, who had promised so easily, and watched as his bulwark deserted him, leaving him to slide down the windshield and thump his gasoline-soaked legs over the side of the blue fender all alone.

"Come-on-a-my house, a my-a-house . . . ," Jack Samuels heard above the sirens and the honking horns. "Come-on-a-my house" and he was off with the rest of the hysterical mob. He never even looked back as Trini unfastened the bonds that tied his legs to the lamppost.

Jack just elbowed little kids from his path and kicked aside whatever seeing-eye dogs got in his way. The closer he came to the hub, the more distinct became the throbbing cheer, the very even and very constant clapping, as if to a signal from an as yet unseen conductor.

"Yeah! Yeah," he heard. Some whistling through teeth. An occasional, "Go, baby, *go!*" and he felt his heart sing. If, as it turned out, he was not able to record the sounds of gasoline sparking into flame, at least it looked like his day wouldn't be a total washout. He was sure that at the end of this crowded rainbow there would be some sort of treasure to get down on the tapes.

He pushed onward, the crowd around him swaying to the steady pulse of a Negro spiritual, but now there was something else . . . a distinctly new throb, which he found quite expressive, though he couldn't as yet translate its origin.

"There he goes," Trini meanwhile was moaning, all alone. All absolutely forgotten and alone up on the Kaiser, where he was busy crapping extensively into his pants. But for the first time since the Board of Education did their job on him, Trini felt perfectly contented. He didn't mind sitting there with gas pains and his diarrhea sloshing around in his boxer shorts. There was something quite soothing about it. He leaned back against the windshield and realized that in his entire life, only this sudden disgorging of his lower sphincter had ever given him a sense of security. Something he could count on. What did he care if the rest of the world ran down the street after false prophets? He had the squishing caress around his privates to snuggle up against.

He dropped the book of matches into the gutter and looked through the belly of the crowd to bid a final farewell to Jack Samuels, that golden man, that friend in need, for whom had it been possible, he would have crossed his Rubicon forever. Only he couldn't find him, long since had he been digested by the man-eating mob. Long since had he forgotten his one-time protégé.

Jack Samuels had other problems . . . as he stood with wide-open mouth and closed eyes. For there, in the dead center of this entire tumult, he could now quite clearly make out the body of none other than his very own wife. His errant very own wife, who no longer, it seemed, suffered from that old ringing between her legs. Who, on top of a city bus, lay on her back busily taking on all comers. Ex-tamale stuffers, seventh-grade hooky-players, off-duty mailmen, and even the cowboy-booted Kotex salesman, who hadn't had a piece for eleven months . . . and she was moaning and writhing in a kind of tear-stained exultation because it was also her eighteenth birthday. "Happy birthday to me," he seemed to hear her moan in between groans . . . "Happy birthday to me," as she fornicated her twat down to the grizzle.

"I have miscalculated," Jack realized as his old raspberry rash came rushing out all over his scrotum clear down the insides of his thighs to the middle of his knee.

As his lovely bride of such short duration shrieked lasciviously, just before she passed out from exhaustion with her head in between a pair of tweed legs.

"Ivory Soap for President!" she called, "oh, Mary, mother of us all, *Ivory Soap for President.* . . . Praise the Lord!!"

· 45 ·

BUT THE SINS OF THE DAUGH-
ter Jack was determined to visit on the mother, as she
writhed in ecstasy under his naked body. He rubbed the
palm of his hand around her breast as far as it would
go in one direction and then turned the motion around
the other way. The other hand, much as it disgusted
him, was stuck as far as it would go into her dripping
hole. She had her legs wrapped so tightly around him,
squeezing him in even further, that he had all he could
do not to puke and spoil everything. She moaned and
slurped, bathing his ears, the inside of his mouth, and
the hair all over his chest. She pressed her unoccupied
breast against his chest, where it flattened against him
all soft and mushy, just the way she loved it.

Her husband now safely tucked away in the nut-house, Dell Collins, as well as her daughter, went at it claw and tongue. In one day she'd had everybody from the neighborhood, including transients, truck drivers, and the Sunday school teacher from up the block . . . but nobody like her gorgeous son-in-law, oh velvet and satin. Oh hair and flesh.

The pink mule on her veiny foot banged back and forth against her heel as Jack closed his eyes tightly, thought about razor blades, and sucked away at one breast after another. . . . No matter what he had to do, he was determined to finally even things up in his ledger. But Dell Collins, in her best almond-colored negligee, just bit and licked his body that tasted better than roast pork.

He pulled back and watched her lying there with her purple box pulsing with palsy. Her nipples cutting through the air like steel belts. Her belly hard. The teeth in her snatch clawing him. *Now*. Now, she wanted him, carrots, corncobs, fists, old Coke bottles. . . . Anything, she begged, thrashing around this way and that. Thrashing and moaning, as she lay there snapping her pussy all dripping with rotting honey.

"Fuck me!" she screamed. "Now . . . lover mine, come fuck me hard and mean, come fuck me till I bleed. . . ."

But this was the moment Jack had been waiting for. The moment he had martyred himself against her soft flesh about. The moment of ultimate momentum, where there was no going back no matter what . . . her eyes bigger than soup plates. . . . *"Now!"* she screamed again and he jumped up out of bed as if it were a hot stove.

"Fat chance!" he screamed, laughing hysterically. "That'll be the day!! Oh, I'll fuck you, all right," he taunted, holding his sides to keep them from splitting, "I'll fuck you in your good right eye."

And then he watched her. As she hiked herself back off the pillow she'd folded up under her hips. As she opened her eyes and realized what had so firmly hit her.

"Now what are you going to do?" he howled at her. "Now what, you dirty old whore? Like mother, like bitch," he yowled, and rolled on the floor and banged his legs up and down, jumping and flapping his arms around, doing the dance John Huston did in *Treasure of Sierra Madre* ("So you think you've found gold??!!!!" from foot to foot).

"No," she moaned, at first. "No, you can't do this to me." Sitting up and finally throwing herself at his mercy. "You can't do this to me, like daughter, like me . . . can't you see I need it? I need it!" she screamed and held her hand over her snatch so the throbbing wouldn't give her a headache. "Have a heart," she begged him. "I need it!!!" But he only laughed.

"You bastard," she called him. "You mother-fucking bastard," which really struck his funny bone.

And he laughed and he laughed and he laughed so hard that neither of them heard the front door open. Or the door to the bedroom, either.

"You stink!" she was shouting. "You abso-fucking-lutely stink on hot ice, I hate you. . . ." Which was just about when Jack's daddy, Martin W., bowed to the lady and tipped his hat to his son.

"Is that any way for a lady to talk?" he said. Then he added, "Allow me to introduce myself, Ma'am . . . ," which was just before he fell down on top of her and finished up what his son had started, while his son sat there calmly in the chair by the bed, sucking on the end of his thumb.

· 46 ·

> My fire I must kindle
> With chips gathered round,
> And boil my own coffee
> Without being ground.

Billy sang.

The streamers of glittering moon played with the gold in his hair as he opened the window in his room at Holy Innocents' Hospital, climbed out onto the ledge, and jumped from the fifth to the third-floor roof, where he then shimmied the rest of the way down the Blessed Virgin.

> I wash in a pool and I
> Wipe on a sack . . . I carry
> My wardrobe all on my back.

First he lay on his bed and pulled out his belly stitches with his nails, bleeding only slightly. Then he pasted the stitches on his chart with a bit of surgical tape as a farewell memento for the nun with the tweezed face. But before even leaving his stitches, Billy made the rounds of every lavatory in the Intensive Care Unit, also the private baths and Personnel Only ladies' room in OB, Recovery, and Contagious Diseases, collecting the used ends of soap . . . all Ivory. These he stored in his pillowcases, which, when he made his escape, he carried over his shoulder like a hobo.

Billy had finally seen the light darkly through the downy cheeks of his rear end. When his feet hit the sidewalk, they moved with definite vision. Gone was his aimless wanderlust. He half-sprinted, as Father Flanagan had once before him done, also Stanley and/or Livingstone, before even Father Flanagan. Off like his predecessors to brave foreign shores, off to where perhaps he, too, might colonize the heathen. His eyes wet, fear couched comfortably in his heart, ecstasy in his loins, Billy Dawson moved on with confidence. For Jack Samuels had made of Billy a man, not only of purpose, but of parts!

· 47 ·

IT LOOKED LIKE IT WAS CUR-
tains for Jack Samuels' ledger. But Ron Harkness and
Lester Newbauer had already been set in motion. Nothing Jack could do or undo could have slowed down
their particular momentum.

"You can come out now," Lester called to Ron, who
hid in the back seat on the floor, where he kept falling
asleep from the exhaust fumes that rose up through a
crack in the muffler. The horizon stretched out around
them like an encephalograph, the mountains already
turned to dusk.

"Come on," Lester begged him, still not exactly sure
why his lover had run into the living room waving his
arms around in shock.

"Him . . . him," he shrieked, "the one with the motorcycle," and it wasn't till they'd hit Route 52 that Les realized he was talking about Jack Samuels.

I wonder what happened, Lester wondered as Ron came to, sat up, and said, *"Easy Street? Where has it gone to?"*

The ruin of Chaco Canyon lay in a haze against the purple evening, and from the ranger's house all Lester could see was a flicker of light tickling the night like a conductor's flashlight in an abandoned railroad station. It was enough humanity to keep Ron down on the floor till they drove up behind the ruin itself and could see nothing but stars.

"Chaco Canyon?" Lester had said. "We're not scheduled to go till Friday!" Ron threw cans, onions, and Tabasco into a cardboard box and foamed at the mouth.

They left so quickly and so hurriedly they forgot the boiled chicken for Lester. They forgot the knife and they forgot the extra blankets, but what else was there for it? Ron Harkness looked like he had seen Hamlet's father, and he'd turned out to be a lesbian.

"C'mon," Lester said, again, this time when he parked, "We're here, and you have to come out sometime. Tell me what happened." But Ron still couldn't talk about it. He couldn't quite sift it out himself, Mrs. Whatever climbing the walls in his office. The blinking yellow light at the corner of Menaul and Lomas. The screaming Jack Samuels running ahead, always out of reach and ruining everything so easily.

"I don't want to talk about it," he said again, the

corners of his eyes ringed with orange. "I just don't want to talk about it at all," and when Lester drew him into his arms, he could feel a low belly-shaking that rippled over the psychological counselor's entire body down as far as his in-grown toenail.

"O.K.," Lester said tenderly, "at least now we're both on the wrong side of zero. Lean on me, what else can happen?" He laid a hand on Ron's bald spot, helped him out of the car into the night that smelled of pinion, and together, little by little, they unpacked everything they needed for their getaway.

"What do we care?" Lester crooned. "You and me are going to fuck by firelight. You and me are going to have us a big pot of chili, a night under the stars, and the whole world to ourselves.

"Come on," he said, and took his lover's hand. "Come on, baby," helping him on with his sheepskin bombardier jacket and his hat with the matching earflaps, "Come on, baby, you know me . . . at least I'll never say I told you so."

They moved quickly. It was turning dark fast. Ron sighed. He stood a minute and sighed again. "Oh God," he moaned, but Lester stopped him. "I'm hungry," he said, "you can suffer later."

Ron went in terror for the kindling. Lester cut the onions, peeled the carrots, and wondered.

The fire burned low. Lester poured on the marjoram.

"What can he do to you?" he said, shaking in some coriander. "You're the one with the Ph.D. Who do you think they're going to believe?" But somehow when Ron looked back at the blinking yellow lights and the honking trucks and the shopkeepers staring at him through their plate glass windows, he wasn't so sure.

"You can make yourself a hamburger," he said.

"Sure I can," Lester said, tasting the sauce and then throwing in some more chili peppers.

Lester's ears burned with the cold and the end of his nose was damp. The smell of the bubbling vegetables gave him the kind of thrill he used to have when he used to walk down the street with Joyce. When they used to all look at him and say, there he goes, the man with the girlfriend.

He threw in four more cloves of garlic. Tonight was a night for a banquet. Tomorrow was plenty of time to think about a rape charge against a middle-aged queen, by a two-timing home-wrecker.

"Come on," he said, again and again and again. "Come on," rubbing the tight cords up the back of Ron's neck. "Come on," as they slid into their sleeping bags and waited for the feast to smother the night with aroma. "Come on," he said, "let's do things. Things and more things until our sauce is as thick as a Havasupi love potion. Until we're ready to gorge ourselves with ambience and wash it down with chianti. Come on," with their matching bombardier jackets under their heads like pillows.

Later Lester stuffed the very last dregs into his mouth and then wiped out the pot with *biscocho*. He washed it down with wine, leaned back, wiped his mouth on the back of his hand, and belched a long, contented belch into the night. Pueblo Bonito . . . one hundred miles from nowhere. From Zuni, Mesa Verde, Hopi, Gallup. No matter which way you looked there was never anything between Chaco Canyon and anywhere. They were alone. Just Lester and his love, and Jack the Ruiner was nowhere to be seen.

"Fantastic," Lester sighed. "Fantastic meal, fantastic stars, fantastic you. I'm happy. It's so, so beautiful. I couldn't be, I don't care about this morning, right now, this minute, I couldn't be happier."

"In about half an hour you're going to sludge down three jars of Gelusil," Ron answered him, laying his head in his lap.

"Uh huh, but right now, this particular minute, with you and me . . . Hey, sweetheart," Lester crooned. "Throw another log on our fire and then come right back, don't waste a minute.

"Aren't you happy? Tell me," he begged, squeezing out the sudden memory of his recent destitution. "Tell me you've never been happier either."

They moved the bed rolls closer to the fire, peed against twin scrub pines, wriggled down exhausted inside, already huddling together to keep out the cold. The wind was clean and pure frost as it drove the men's eyes further and further under the sleeping bag. Lester was already asleep, beads of garlic sweat coating his forehead. Ron pulled him closer and closer against his chest. "Yes," he whispered with abandon. "Yes, I'm happy. Yes, this minute, whatever happens, I've never in my whole Porky Pig life been happier." And then, quite suddenly, two hours later, when they were both deep in the depths of solid sleep, Lester jolted upright as if goosed.

"What's the . . . ?" Ron asked him through the distance. Then a roar more torrential than Hurricane Arlene. A terrible, rhythmic lurching hiccup that burst from the center of Lester's bottommost center of gravity. A sudden tidal wave bursting forth over and over again. Hot and greasy, still fuming with aroma. . . . Chili, onions, potatoes, carrots, turnips, parsnips, celery, leeks, pork, tomatoes, tortillas, and even whole unchewed chili pods. Some guts, some stomach. It poured out of him.

"Oh, my God," he murmured through the wine-colored avocados. It drove out, pushed out, gushed out all over them, all over the sleeping bag, all over everything, mixed with bile and a new unearthly odor more foul than death.

Ron sat up and watched as the stuff kept coming, as it stopped only long enough for Lester to breathe and then started again, long after there couldn't possibly have been any more food, and then more, more food and more insides. More something, in the darkness under the flickering coal glow from the dead fire. Bits of Jack Samuels' Fritos, coriander, Pastoso, and small intestine. A marjoram geyser of pulsing heat.

They were drenched, soaked in vomit. In the awful stink and decay. In the smell, as Lester grabbed his body with both arms and rolled his eyes back into his head.

"My pills," he moaned. He jerked an arm towards

the Hudson. "My pills, the little green pills. Oh, my God," he hollered, "dear God, help me, I promise I'll never do it again...."

Ron, for a moment, couldn't move. He had to get the pills, the little green pills. He knew he shouldn't have let Lester eat chili. Wasn't he going to eat a hamburger? What little green pills? and then he ran. He jumped, he tore, he threw open the door on the silver car and buried his terror in a frantic search for the little green Sebella that he was going to what? Force upstream like salmon? Up Lester's downward torrent?

Lester was afraid to talk. His throat ached from retch. Bits and chunks of everything clung to his tonsils, and the pain began to be worse than he could have ever imagined. He lay back in a pool of reeking stew. It was cold, thick, and runny with blood. He opened his eyes wide in the pitch black and realized what was happening to him. His mouth opened again and more came, now mostly blood. Pure, hot, gushing blood, pouring out of him, foodless, vomitless. He passed out.

Ron opened his mouth and tried the pills, but on the next geyser they spurted out along with the hotter, purer blood. Ron drew his hands off and a scream of fear and anguish tore from his bowels and scored the air. He stood immobile holding Lester's body in his arms as the next gush of hot blood bathed them both. And then he moved. He jerked the bleached-white Lester to his feet and dragged him to the car, while he retched gallons, acres, rivers of life. Hemorrhaging, suffocating the canyon so that it looked like a sacrificial altar to the God of Retribution. He left the embers, the pots, the bed rolls, the sweaters soaked in blood, and their twin sheepskin-lined bombardier jackets. He forced Lester's inert body into the death seat and ran around to the wheel even though he couldn't drive. This was not the time for *couldn't* and it was all a question of pushing the right knobs and pulling the right sticks. He'd seen it done enough. It would have to do.

First he couldn't find the keys and had to force his hands down Lester's pockets. Then the car bleated like a kid, jerked, choked, and lurched into and then out of gear. The stick wouldn't move. He couldn't get it to cooperate, and beside him, his lover's head balanced a moment on the end of his neck and then fell to the side so that it cracked the window with a thud. Ron took a long breath and told himself that panicking would get him nowhere. He told himself to remember the two lessons he'd had in driver education class so he could graduate high school. And finally he remembered what you had to do to get the stick down into neutral. He remembered, he did it, and he closed his eyes so he could visualize what he had to know to get them up and out of the canyon.

It made a funny sound. Hurting almost, as it suffered up the winding road, but after six false starts he did do it. He got into one of the gears, which he couldn't quite remember, but he did get them up to the highway and then turned in one of the directions toward one of the destinations one hundred miles away. He could have gone to the ranger, but he didn't think of him. He could have looked at a map, but all he did was drive. He turned left, because it seemed right, and he pressed his foot down on the gas as far as it would go.

Lester wasn't through bleeding. Through his sleep, he'd burp every so often, and the seeping blood poured out of his mouth and sometimes even his nose. Ron would lay a hand on his shoulder and press his foot down even harder, though he noticed that when the speedometer measured eighty, the car began to sound like a coffee can filled with cement nails.

After a while he allowed himself another glance at the dashboard, where he noticed they didn't have much gas, but his hands held the steering wheel so hard they had turned white to his wrists. There was a faint rim of haze in the distance and then there wasn't. He allowed himself the luxury of changing the subject. What, he allowed himself to wonder, was it? A light in somebody's bathroom? A snipe hunt?

He lived again his chase down Menaul across Lomas and why practically a total stranger had gone out of his way to ruin everything. No, not everything. Everything lay next to him in the death seat bleeding all over the crankshaft.

The flat miles and continuous desert bellowed through his ears while Lester slept. Sometimes he thought Lester said something, and sometimes he thought they'd even make it. But the sound of his lover's voice came through a wash of wet tongue, and the needle on the gas gauge fell nearer and nearer to nowhere.

And then Lester woke with a jerking start. He groaned with pain, said quite clearly, "You were right," after which he began a feeble mimicry of the earlier violent vomiting. He was cold and his blood all over him was making him shiver. Ron said they were doing fine. He said, "Go to sleep, we're almost there." If he slept he couldn't vomit so much. "Go to sleep," he begged him. "Baby," he said. "Go to sleep, baby, everything's going to be fine."

It looked like he did, the way his head jerked around loose like it did, but it didn't stop the vomiting. He just puked and retched and vomited more and more blood. Gently, with his mouth kind of hanging open and the continuous leak bleating out like a metronome. And through it all, Ron felt himself falling asleep. Even after the haze of light turned to a faint pool of concentrated light. Even after it had turned into a Conoco station. Even after he pulled in almost close enough to the pump, banged on the door of the little house next to the darkened station, and woke up the lady, who kept a night light on because she was afraid of the dark.

· 48 ·

MORT AND ASHLEY DRALON
called their second son Solomon, in hopes. They moved
to Veracruz, because Thalia had a summer home there
that she wanted to rent. Mort thought that for a
mother-in-law she charged them rather a lot, but Ashley said, wouldn't he ever learn to adjust to the way her
family did things, and under the circumstances, Mort
felt he had to go along. Rhile's arms had been long since
set back in their sockets and everything was turning out
just swell, except, of course, that the doctor had told
them the boy would never play baseball. But then,
athletics weren't everything to a good Jewish boy, and
the specialist didn't say anything about his never playing the violin.

· 49 ·

was a poignant one, beginning, as it did, at the site of his almost-immolation, and including his subsequent marriage to Amy Collins. (Her first brief alliance having long since been annulled.) Yes, it was there, on the fender of a midnight-blue Kaiser, that the thought first came to Trini that what the world really needed was neither another mousetrap nor a teacher of band instruments. What it needed, it became quite evident, was a fire extinguisher that would fit comfortably in the carrying case for a bugging device. And on this insight he built his success.

Dripping with gasoline, he jumped off the fender, walked by the haunting moans of his future wife, on top of her bus and underneath the entire seventh grade from Nob Hill Junior High, and went home to his lonely room to invent his fire extinguisher from old tamale cans, worn-down rubber heels, and Mexican-American know-how. Then he peddled them door to door in a false mustache and threw in a free Bible, which proved to be such an unbeatable combination he became a millionaire in eighteen months, which was just about the time Senator Joseph McCarthy received his comeuppance.

It was then Trini took off his mustache, once more showed his true colors, and became the darling of the Young Radicals (plus the chastened Board of Education), now anxious to mend their old misbegotten ways on the front page of *The Daily Herald*.

But that, too, passed. The Young Radicals got him down off their shoulders as his fortunes rose and the intervening sixties intervened. But still Trini held his tongue, as if he knew in his heart that the seventies, too, would come.

As they did. Finding Congress, as Trini knew they would, debating not whether or not Athens should or shouldn't have given old Socrates the hemlock, but rather, when they should commemorate the momentous moment. When exactly they should declare the day of his execution the nation's latest national holiday. When, to the hour, the actual historical precedent had taken place.

The Southern Dixiecrats insisted it was the Ides of October, while the extreme left-wing coalition hung out for the cold winds of February. But in either case, it was inevitable that Trinidad Lucero and his insatiable wife Amy, should spend their declining years in the comfort of one governor's mansion or another, when they were not otherwise being cradled in the bosoms of their respective families.

Nor could it, in the Golden Land of Opportunity, have turned out otherwise.